Ellen Elizabeth Hawkins

MOBEETIE, TEXAS, 1886

—⸻—

by Kathleen Duey

—⸻—

Aladdin Paperbacks

For Richard
For Ever

25 *Years of Magical Reading*

ALADDIN PAPERBACKS
EST. 1972

First Aladdin Paperbacks edition, April 1997
Copyright © 1997 by Kathleen Duey

Aladdin Paperbacks
An imprint of Simon & Schuster
Children's Publishing Division
1230 Avenue of the Americas
New York, NY 10020

The text of this book was set in Fairfield Medium.
Printed and bound in the United States of America
10 9 8 7 6 5 4 3 2 1

Library of Congress Cataloging-in-Publication Data
Duey, Kathleen.
Ellen Elizabeth Hawkins : Mobeetie, Texas, 1886 / Kathleen
Duey. — 1st Aladdin Paperbacks ed.
p.   cm. — (American diaries ; #6)
Summary: In Texas in 1886, Ellen finds her desire to be a cattle
rancher discouraged by family members who do not think it a
proper choice for a girl, but she proves her worth when drought
threatens the ranch.
ISBN 0-689-81409-7
[1. Ranch life—Texas—Fiction. 2. Texas—Fiction. 3. Sex
role—Fiction. 4. Droughts—Fiction.] I. Title. II. Series.
PZ7.D8694Ej   1997
[Fic]—dc21   96-39818
CIP   AC

No rain yet. Almost no wind.

I have not written for four days—there are simply too many chores with Pa gone. I am on the porch to write this and it is hot even now, after supper at nine thirty. Both windmills stood still as stones all day. The stock tank west of the house is only half full—the one in the east pasture is probably low as well. I will check it first thing tomorrow. Grampa and I had to pull a calf this morning. The mama cow lived. I think they will both be all right. It took hours, and we fell behind on all else. Grampa says the calvings are troublesome because of the drouth.

The grass is burning up under the sun. Grampa says he has never seen it this dry. He is worried about his favorite mare, Fay. Her foal should come soon. We brought her up to the barn and put her in the stall with the milk cow three days ago.

Pa was angry and worried when he rode out with the cattle. I know he was wishing, as he always has, that he had a son to leave things to, or even a hired man. Once he was over the rise and on his way, I ran back to the barn and cried for so long that Grampa came out. How shamed I was. Crying like a baby.

Pa had to go. I know that and I am not scared to have him gone a few days. I only cried because so much is bad this year. The cattle are weary and thin from the drouth—Grampa says we might just have a real die-up before it rains. I pray we won't. I have heard stories of cattle dropping from thirst—and horses—with their tongues black and swollen. Deerfoot whinnied just now from the barn, as though she could read my thoughts.

Pa took fifty head of cattle to sell, about half the herd, yearlings, steers, and barren cows. He says it's better to let the JA boys drive our cattle north to Dodge with theirs than watch them die here. All the ranches are selling off stock, of course, even the Frying Pan, the XIT, and Colonel Goodnight at the JA. So the prices will go even farther down.

These four days since Pa left, chores have kept my hands flying, and my feet. Grampa worked with me. We sang old trail songs, were laughing today. Pa always works silent. He would not like the way Grampa and I do things, but the jobs get done. Pa should be back late tomorrow. I don't think he can find fault with the way I've done the work. The Hereford bull he bought from Colonel Goodnight was looking a little rough yesterday. All the stock is poor from the drouth, but if anything happens to that bull, Pa will disown me.

The stars are bright tonight. Too bright. If only it would rain. I watch the sky all the time, hoping, but it is endlessly blue, endlessly hot. I saw a shooting star just now, a beauty, with a tail like a spray of dew flung from a lark's wing. It will rain someday. I only hope it rains before everything dries up and dies. How much longer can we last?

CHAPTER ONE

Ellen wiped the nib of her steel pen and set it back in the inkwell. Then she blew on the page, waiting until the faint shine disappeared on the long, slanted letters she had written. It took only a few seconds. The air was warm and dry.

Ellen took a long breath and closed her diary. She loved writing in it. In fact, she loved the book itself. It had been her mother's. The first ten pages were filled with neat, small penmanship—Ellen's mother's account of the first year on this ranch, when she and Ellen's father were working so hard they often fell asleep in their clothes, too tired to undress for bed.

Ellen had read those precious pages a hundred times; they had been written before she was born, when her mother had been just eighteen, scared, but determined to be a good ranch wife.

The diary's tan cover was worn and faded, and the leather tie was frayed—the diary had been at the bottom of her mother's trunk for two years before Ellen discovered it. Ellen was twelve now. Her mother had died when she was eight.

Ellen slid the diary beneath the wooden chair, then leaned back, lifting her heavy blond braid so it swung down behind the backrest. She shut her eyes. It was perfectly dark and perfectly quiet tonight. Grampa had gone to bed right after supper. Tired from doing more work than he was used to, he had lain down on his cot, still dressed, pulled his sugar-loaf hat over his eyes, and fallen asleep.

So Ellen had lit the lantern and come out onto the porch to write in her diary. In the morning, she promised herself, she would think of some easy chore for Grampa. He was going to overwork himself right into a sickbed if he wasn't careful. She smiled, thinking about how he had bustled around all day, teaching her little tricks and shortcuts for almost every job they'd done. Ellen liked to listen to him whistling while he worked.

Ellen was thirsty, but she would wait awhile

before she went in to get a dipperful of water from the bucket on the sideboard. Grampa slept on a hard cot in the big room and any commotion at all would wake him, even as tired as he was. He had been a cowboy most of his life, sleeping with one ear pricked up and one eye half open. He had taken longhorn cattle up the trail to Kansas back in the days when there were no fences, no soldiers, no Texas Rangers to keep things in order.

Ellen looked out at the night. The darkness began at the foot of the porch stairs and went on across the yard, filling the house pasture. It was dark all the way across Indian Territory, all the way to places like New York and Boston—places she had never seen and probably never would see.

Ellen stared at nothing, resting. There was no one within ten miles, most likely, unless a stray cowboy had drifted away from one of the ranches and camped overnight in some gully beyond the ranch fences. The fences had taken three years for her father to build. The work was hard, but the cost of the cedar fence posts had slowed him down, too. Ellen had liked helping to build the fences—she had liked the trips into Mobeetie to get the fence posts, too. They rarely went to town except for supplies.

Every third post in their fences was cedar,

freighted in to Mobeetie from the cedar brakes in Indian Territory. The two in between were native, Panhandle cottonwood, hauled in from the nearest creek bottom. They would rot sooner, but they cost only time and labor, two things her father had more of than money.

Ellen had heard about people who hated the fencing, who came in the night and cut the wire over and over, as fast as the ranchers could fix it. Some of the cutters had been arrested by Texas Rangers. There had been killings over it. Now Colonel Goodnight was arguing in the courts—they couldn't seem to work out a lease price on public lands. But most of the trouble was farther south, not up here in the Panhandle country, and Ellen was grateful. This drouth was trouble enough.

Ellen closed her eyes, then opened them, startled at a sudden whispering rustle in the weeds along the edge of the porch.

A broad, heavy-bodied cat emerged from the drouth-stunted leaves. "Good evening, Spencer," Ellen said, smiling. Spencer meowed, padding across the rough planks to stand at her feet. Ellen slid her ankles forward, making an easy stairway of her legs. She watched the big gray and white tomcat as he leapt up gracefully. Spencer's loud, insistent purr made her smile again. He circled in her

lap, rising to his hind legs to rub his whiskered muzzle against Ellen's sunburned cheek.

"Spencer, you are neglecting Murphy, cozying
up to me like this. She doesn't like for you to leave
her alone." Ellen sat up and looked past the pool of
amber light cast by the lantern. Murphy was probably close by, but Ellen knew she wouldn't show herself. Murphy was a half-wild barn cat, a recluse who
preferred solitude to tidbits, her shy safety to ear-
rubbing and sweet talk. But she adored Spencer,
and would wait, hidden in the bushes, until he was
finished with the human creatures he loved—even
though they terrified her.

"But Murphy catches three mice to every one
of yours, Mister Lazy Bones," Ellen said sweetly to
Spencer. He nuzzled her again, lifting his broad,
gray-masked face. His chin was gray, but a smooth
snow-white bib spread down his chest. And it was
his chest he wanted Ellen to scratch now. She pre-
tended not to understand. "Spencer?" She bunched
her brows like Mrs. Handers at the Mercantile
Store in Mobeetie always did, as though everything
in the world was a big puzzle that needed figuring.
"Spencer, whatever do you want?"

Spencer meowed.

"And do you think it will ever rain again?"
Ellen asked him. The big tomcat stretched, arching

his back and letting the tiniest tip of his claws show, just for an instant. Then he purred louder and raised his chin again.

Ellen stiffened her spine, imitating Mrs. Hander's corseted posture and genteel expression. "And do you think, Mister Spencer, that it will rain again before the world dries up and blows away?"

Spencer wriggled, curving his body, meowing, impatient with Ellen's teasing. He butted her arm with the flat, warm top of his head. Ellen's smile pulled painfully at the split in her lower lip and she let it fade. She licked at the bloody crack. The dry wind made her chap something terrible lately. She would have to rub some beeswax on her lips before she went to bed. Beeswax had been her mother's cure for everything.

"Is Murphy going to have kittens?" Ellen asked while Spencer kneaded her arm with his wide, white paws. "I caught a glimpse of her the other day and she looked like she was in the family way." Spencer's purr rumbled deep in his throat. "Maybe she will have four or five gray and white little tom-cats, and you can lead your sons around and show everyone how proud you are of them."

"He'll be just as proud if Murphy has a litter of brown tabbies that look like their mother," Grampa said from the doorway. "Or he ought to be. Murphy is the finest mouser in Wheeler County, maybe in the whole Texas Panhandle."

Ellen turned, almost knocking the inkwell off the porch rail. "I thought you went to bed, Grampa."

"Too hot to sleep. I'm thinking about bringing my old soogans out here and spreading a bedroll under the sky."

"Grampa," Ellen chided him, teasing. "Sleeping outside when you can have a bed indoors?"

Grampa snorted, his grizzled chin wrinkling, his yellowed teeth showing as he laughed. "Me, odd?" He teased back. "Says who? You? Out here talking to cats, for spit's sake. Conversing with tomcats beneath the stars." He ran a hand back through his gray, wiry hair, turning serious. "This is no proper life for a girl."

Ellen didn't answer. This was an old argument. Two or three times a year Grampa and her father would go on a stampede about her wearing her father's hand-me-down work pants instead of skirts and riding astride instead of using a sidesaddle. But the truth was she hated skirts. They got in the way of ranch work. And she liked talking to animals. They were her friends.

"No one sees me except you and Pa anyway," she said aloud, to head him off before he got started. "And Deerfoot hates that sidesaddle."

Ellen Elizabeth Hawkins   11

"Well, you're getting older now," Grampa said, looking up at the sky. "Couple, three years, you'll be old enough to start courting. Then what? You going to explain to your sweetheart that you look like a boy 'cause your daddy and grampa kept you ranching instead of learning something about being a lady?"

Ellen shook her head. "I don't want a sweetheart. I want to raise cattle like you and Pa."

Grampa snorted again, this time in disapproval. "A woman can't be a cow man. It ain't right." He reached down and picked up Spencer, rubbing the cat's chest briskly. Spencer purred louder and cast a slit-eyed glance of disdain at Ellen. His meaning was plain as daylight. Grampa's chest rubs were wonderful, and Spencer did not have to beg.

"What about Mrs. Adair?" Ellen asked. "She runs her ranch."

Grampa gave her a sidelong look. "It's different. She's a widow."

"She does a good job, though, doesn't she?"

Grampa was silent for a long time. "I suppose," he said finally, so softly that she could barely hear. Grampa set Spencer down. "It's time you started acting like a lady, Ellen."

"That's what Pa thinks, too," Ellen said quietly. She felt a familiar tightness starting in her belly. If she had been a boy, everything would be different. Her father would be proud of the way she could ride any-thing with four legs and a tail, not ashamed. He'd want her to practice roping a fence post, not scold her for it. He'd show her off, not shoo her into the house whenever anyone rode up with business to talk.

"You can't be what you ain't, Ellen." Grampa laid his hand on her shoulder, then lifted her braid to tug it once, gently, his bony fingers warm and rough where they brushed her neck.

Her thoughts scattered by his touch, Ellen watched him cross the porch, clumping unevenly down the steps to stand in the yard. He craned back, looking up at the night sky. After a minute, he looked over his shoulder at her. "Dry as a bone. But maybe tomorrow it'll cloud up. Heard rooster racket a full hour too early this morning. That can mean a change in the weather."

Ellen nodded, hearing the note of hope in his voice. Spencer leapt into her lap, and she rubbed his ears absently. A faint sound from off to the west made Ellen look past Grampa. He turned, too, lift-ing his hand to shade his eyes as though the sun were blinding him, not the dark of night.

"What is it?" Ellen whispered.

Grampa tilted his head and spoke without turning. "Trouble."

Ellen Elizabeth Hawkins   13

CHAPTER TWO

Ellen stood, letting Spencer slide gently to the floor. He meowed, but she ignored him, her eyes fixed on Grampa's back. He was absolutely still, every part of his body rigid with the effort to listen.

When Grampa stood at attention like this, the crookedness of his stance was emphasized. A lifetime on horseback had worn out his knees and shaped his legs to fit a cowboy's saddle. Ellen thought about the rank-tempered longhorn that had shattered Grampa's legs, had narrowly missed killing him. It had happened twenty years before, and Grampa had been stove up off and on since.

His legs had never stopped aching. Nor had they healed evenly.

Ellen had never known her grandfather when he was straight and tall. His odd, off-balance walk was part of him. So was his amazing hearing. Even now, at seventy-four years old, he often heard the hoofbeats of approaching visitors before anyone else did.

"What is it, Grampa?" Ellen whispered the question. He raised a hand to shush her, but didn't answer. Ellen strained, but couldn't hear anything. The silence had closed in as completely as the darkness had. Seconds ticked past. Spencer meowed again, pushing himself against her shin so hard that he rose up on his hind legs. Ellen reached down automatically and rubbed his head, her eyes still fixed on the direction the sound had come from.

"Do you hear anything now?" Grampa asked, as she had, in a whisper.

"No."

He turned, his boots gritting on the sandy soil. "It's a ways off, but it's mama cows bawling, and I don't like the sound of it." Ellen wanted to ask how he knew it had been cows with calves bawling—not steers or the Hereford bull—but she didn't. She watched him as he turned to face her. "If your pa was here, he'd ride out to have a look."

Ellen nodded.

Grampa hitched his bandanna straight, pushing the little bone slide up the stained red silk to tighten it around his throat. "Once the moon comes up, I'll ride down to the east pasture and take a look." He pointed at the horizon, and for the first time Ellen noticed a blue-gray half circle shading the edge of the black sky. It silhouetted the wilting leaves of the trumpet vine that covered the porch roof.

Ellen reached down and lifted the lantern, swinging it in a small quick circle to feel the weight of the kerosene in its metal reservoir. It was nearly full. "Let's get saddled up and by then . . ."

"There is no 'let's' about this, Ellen," Grampa interrupted her. "You ain't coming with me."

"What if it's a wolf or . . ."

"If it is a wolf, I'll run it off. It won't come back tonight, and I'll ride it down in the morning."

Ellen blinked. Grampa rarely rode at all anymore. It hurt his knees to ride, and they were already aching from the extra work he was doing. Her father would never allow him to hunt wolves alone. "What if something happens and . . ."

"It won't," Grampa said. "I'll be as careful as a cat in a room full of rocking chairs." Spencer meowed again and rubbed against Ellen's leg.

Grampa laughed. "He thinks we're talking with him. He's got so used to your conversation, he even answers me." He went inside and came back out, wearing his sugar-loaf hat.

Ellen opened her mouth to speak, but Grampa held up one hand. "You ain't going. No arguments. Go get the shotgun for me. Load it."

Ellen hesitated, and he made a shooing motion with his hand. "If the trouble was a wolf, it's gone. But we don't know that. Could be two-legged trouble."

Ellen drew in a quick breath. "Thieves?"

Grampa shrugged his bony shoulders. "Or maybe just strays from someone else's herd leaning on the ribbon wire and bawling about being thirsty. Nothing can smell out water like a longhorn."

"But Grampa—"

"No buts." He pinched each word as it came out of his mouth, his face set and stern. "Light me a lantern. Git."

Ellen whirled and nearly stumbled over Spencer. He meowed indignantly and disappeared into the bushes.

The lanterns were hung in a row just inside the door. Ellen hefted two, then chose the one on the right; it had more fuel. She got down the little iron match safe and struck two matches before she managed to light the wick. Her hands were unsteady, her breathing quick as she carried the lit lantern out onto the porch. "Did you hear anything else?"

Grampa took the lantern from her without answering for a minute, then nodded. "Maybe. I'll start by riding the fenceline down into the east pasture. If everything is all right there, I'll come back up and go out the road gate and ride the fenceline down on the outside. If nothing is amiss anywhere, I'll come home. I won't dawdle."

"Please be careful, Grampa," Ellen said, and she saw his face soften.

"You sound like your mother."

Ellen swallowed. "I just want you safe."

Grampa nodded. "So did she. She was way too good for your father. Just like her mama was way too good for an old cowboy like me."

It was a worn-out family joke, but they both smiled anyway. Grampa didn't talk about his daughter—her mother—very often, and she loved it when he did. Her mother had been a lot like her as a girl—helping on the ranch and good at roping and riding.

"I'll take it real easy," Grampa said. He lifted her braid again and tugged it gently. Then, without saying any more, he swung around and started toward the barn. As always when he was trying to hurry, his gait was even more lopsided than usual.

His left shoulder dipped sharply with every step, echoing the limp that favored his left leg. The lantern swung, moving the shadows as he passed. He crossed the yard toward the barn, the circle of light moving with him. The lantern seemed to wink out as he went behind the chicken coop.

Ellen watched the dimming light from the lantern until the barn door shut and it was gone. Then she went back in, grateful to be surrounded by the glow of honeyed light, protected by the familiar walls of the little house.

The picket walls, covered with blue clay mud and homemade ash-colored whitewash, looked uneven and dingy in the lantern light. Her mother had plastered them herself, just before she had gotten sick. The walls had five years' worth of ranch dust and fly specks on them now.

"We don't know that anything is really wrong," Ellen said aloud as she lifted the rifle from the pair of mounted steer horns that served as a gun rack over the mantle. Her father had taken his six-shooter with him. "It could have been a cow separated from her calf." She loaded the rifle, then turned for the door. On her way out, she put her left hand through the lantern's wire bale, lifting it in a smooth motion without slowing her step.

Spencer followed as she crossed the yard. She

saw a streak of motion from the corner of her eye and knew that Murphy was heading toward the barn, too, probably in hope of a second dish of milk. Ellen had given the cats a treat from the evening milking. She usually did, unless she was bottle-feeding calves and couldn't spare a drop.

Ellen slowed her step a little as she passed the chicken coop, trying not to startle the hens out of their warm-feathered sleep. Her father always said that a hen that was startled awake in the night wouldn't lay the next day. Ellen held her breath for a few seconds to avoid the smell of the drying cattle hides that had been nailed to the side of the chicken coop. The heat had cured them fast. They were already stiff, shrinking so that the nail holes were two-inch tears in the leather. It would be her job to cut them into strips later. They used rawhide for everything.

"Ellen?" It was Grampa's voice, impatient and rough. He wasn't angry, Ellen was sure. His knees probably already hurt from the hurried walk down to the barn.

"Coming!" Ellen gripped the rifle tighter, raised the lantern, and walked faster down the path.

The barn door was ajar. Grampa's lantern cast long shadows on the picket walls. Fay, her blazed sorrel face unnaturally red in the amber light of the lantern, looked over the top rail of her stall. Across the aisle, the mama cow they had helped that morning stood contentedly, her calf nosing at the rail.

Ellen smiled. Grampa was saddling Deerfoot— her mare. Deerfoot looked around nervously at Ellen. She wasn't used to her night's rest being disturbed, and she was even less accustomed to being saddled by this old man who smelled of hair oil and coffee.

"Do you mind my taking your mare?"

"Of course not." Ellen leaned the rifle against the wall near the door and set down the lantern before she went to hold Deerfoot steady. Her father had ridden his paint stallion. Fay was too close to foaling to work and even if she hadn't been, she was a little flighty. The four young geldings out in the corral were barely saddle broke. Deerfoot was by far the gentlest animal on the place and would be least likely to act up and throw him if there was wolf scent on the wind or a sudden motion in the dark.

Ellen winced at the idea of Grampa being bucked off. He had spent most of his life in a saddle. Being thrown would hurt every part of him, including his pride.

Deerfoot's breath was warm and moist against Ellen's cheek. She was big for a mare, a rough-coated bay—not especially pretty. She had a Roman nose, and the skin on her muzzle was mottled pink and gray. But Ellen loved her intelligent eyes, her wide forehead, the flecks of white on her shoulders, the two long white stockings that marked her hind feet.

"Back up a little, Ellen," Grampa said. "Let the mare know it's me that's going to get up in a minute here."

"Yes, Grampa," Ellen murmured, stepping back.

Deerfoot shifted uneasily. "I know you're wondering what in tarnation this is all about," Grampa said soothingly as he slid the cinch tighter, waiting for the instant when Deerfoot let her breath out completely. When she had, he hauled the cinch tight before she could swell her belly with another breath. He adjusted the back cinch to fit snugly against the mare's body, but not as tightly as the first.

Deerfoot stamped a front hoof. She wasn't used to the heavy cinches on Grampa's rimfire, heavy-rigged saddle. The latigo strips on the back of the saddle were long, too, and they hung down and tickled her sides.

"We are mighty sorry to trouble you after supper like this," Grampa told Deerfoot as he tied his riata onto the saddle. The stiff coil of braided rawhide rope was always well oiled and ready for use—even though he almost never used it anymore. When he had been younger, though, he had been a good roper. Sometimes he helped Ellen practice when she roped fence posts.

Grampa led Deerfoot out of the barn. The heavy eagle-bill tapaderos that covered the stirrups swung and touched the mare's sides as she moved. Ellen saw her ears flicker back and forth once more, a crescent of white appearing at the edge of her eyes as she tried to look backward at the saddle that creaked and pinched in unfamiliar places on her back.

Ellen stood silently watching as Grampa struggled to get his left foot in the stirrup. She knew better than to offer to help him. He'd give her what for, and remind her that he'd grown up in a saddle instead of a cradle—and that this saddle, in particular, was as familiar to him as his own hands.

Ellen knew the story of how he had won the saddle in a card game. It had been thirty years before.

"She'll be good, Grampa," Ellen said, mostly just to have something to say. She watched him carefully, trying to look like she wasn't. She was ready to step forward and take the reins, but it wasn't needed. Deerfoot stood very still, only her restless ears twitching, indicating her uneasiness.

Grampa hauled himself up awkwardly, grunting and grimacing. But once he was in the saddle, he settled himself and smiled down at her. "I miss riding a good horse," he said wistfully, then frowned. "But I tell you what—my knees surely don't." He shook his head. "They prefer a good buggy." He touched the brim of his hat. You just don't worry yourself, Little Miss Ellen. I'll be right back. I'll check on Colonel Hereford while I'm down there, too."

Ellen nodded, smiling. Colonel Hereford was Grampa's nickname for the bull her father had bought from Colonel Goodnight. Ellen lifted the lantern for Grampa to take. He shook his head and pointed toward the horizon. "The moon will work as well, and we won't chance a fire." He swung Deerfoot around, then pulled up and called back over his shoulder, "Watch your step going back to the house. It's warm enough to have rattlers crawling tonight."

Ellen nodded; he was right. "You be careful, too."

Deerfoot turned her head, bending around far enough to nose the leather tapaderos. She wasn't used to the heavy stirrup covers. Grampa clucked at her, touching her sides with his heels, starting off. Ellen watched until the darkness made him disappear.

CHAPTER THREE

Ellen started for the house. She held a lantern in each hand, keeping them high so they lit the path in front of her. The wicks had both begun to smoke, soot clouding the glass chimneys. The moment she got inside, Ellen trimmed the wicks with the little steel wick tool and laid it carefully back on the shelf where it was always kept. Then she blew one lantern out. No need to waste oil. She hung it back on its hook beside the door.

Ellen looked around the little house. It wasn't a picket house, exactly, but it wasn't a simple dugout like some of their neighbors had, either. Her parents had cut the straightest cottonwood and hawthorne saplings they could find to build the east wall. They had covered the row of half-buried sapling stakes with clay, smoothing the inside surface just as if it were plaster.

Building that one long wall had used all the sapling trees on their own land, so Ellen's parents had changed plans after talking to a Mexican cowboy who had stopped one night to ask for water for his horse. Following his directions, and using more heavy clay, they had filled square wooden molds with a mixture of the clay and horse manure. The sun had baked the adobes hard.

The north and south walls of the house were built of these adobes, which looked like rough bricks. The west wall was the earth itself. Ellen's parents had dug into the gentle slope that rose, then flattened out again in the two hundred-acre west pasture above the house. The roof was sod, supported by beams made from more young cottonwoods. When it rained very hard, or for a long time, the roof soaked through and leaked. It hadn't rained enough to make it leak in almost two years.

Ellen paced to the hearth and knelt to blow on the ashes. They had used a little wood to cook supper in order to have a bed of coals to heat dishwater afterward. The dried cow dung they usually burned wouldn't hold a coal at all. It burned to a powdery gray ash.

Ellen blew again, adding a piece of wood from the stack of twisted shin oak. She pulled the pot of beans away from the flames that sprang up.

Ellen kept glancing out the open door. The house was small, and although everything in it was familiar, it all looked strange to her tonight. She stared at her father's bed, nearest the door, and tried to recall the last time she had been alone in the house after dark. She couldn't.

As Ellen tended the fire, she was acutely aware of the empty house around her. By dark she was usually playing checkers with her grandfather, or reading one of the books from her mother's trunk while her father and Grampa argued land lease politics or some such issue over steaming cups of coffee. They agreed on very little, and sometimes the arguments got heated. Usually Grampa eased the mood back with a joke or two.

When they did argue long enough to stalk away from each other, Grampa usually went outside. Inside, there was only the main room and the little storeroom, which held their provisions and fresh meat. There was a butchered antelope in it right now. More often, there were prairie chickens her father shot while mending fences or moving cows from one pasture to another.

Pa's and Grampa's rope cots were on the north wall. Ellen's alcove on the opposite wall was separated from the kitchen by blankets her father had hung from the low ceiling beams. Although she was grateful for the privacy the blankets gave her, Ellen sometimes wished she had more.

Every spring her father talked about building another room—one Ellen could have for her own. But every year something kept him too busy, or too worried, or too broke. It had taken everything they had nine years before to buy the 960-acre ranch— a section and a half. Four years ago, they had fenced it into three pastures, side by side, the house pasture in the middle. The cost of the wire and posts had been considerable. Then they'd bought the windmills. Last year, Pa had bought the Hereford bull.

Ellen crossed the room again, nervously glancing at the door. She went to the oak bucket on the counter and lifted the dipper from its hook to get a drink. The water that came from their wells was the sweetest, most wonderful water in the world—even now when the drouth had dried up the creeks and what little water there had been up along the edge of the Llano Estacado.

Ellen drank again. The thought of the Llano

Estacado made her thirsty. She had seen the Staked Plain the year before, from the top of Palo Duro Canyon, riding with her father when he was too short of money to hire to help.

The Llano Estacado was strange country. It was almost waterless—a man and cow killer. Looking out across the vast, flat prairie had made Ellen almost dizzy. The horizon seemed to curve upward instead of lying close to the earth as it should have. As she had ridden behind her father, she'd felt odd, weightless. The arc of the sky soared on and on above them, immense and blue. Clouds had appeared, then spent the whole day moving across that endless sky, scudded along by the constant wind. They had not found their strayed cattle that day. If they had wandered out onto the Llano Estacado, they had probably died of thirst.

Ellen hung up the dipper and blotted her lips on her apron. Then she got down her mother's remedy box. She dug out the little tin of beeswax and held a glob over the glowing coals for a few seconds to soften it. She smeared the wax onto her chapped lips, rubbing them together, the rough scabs grating against each other painfully.

Outside, Ellen heard a sigh of wind in the dry weeds. It'd be good if it blew so the windmills could fill the big earthen tanks, but she was sick of empty wind. It hadn't brought rain all summer, only more heat and drouth. Spencer meowed, and Ellen jumped, startled. "Where did you come from?"

Spencer meowed again, a long, drawn-out sound that seemed to Ellen as though he really were trying to answer in English. He rubbed against her leg, adding a little jig-step to the middle of his passage, his front feet coming off the ground to massage his shoulder and one ear against the cotton cloth of her work pants. Ellen smiled, knowing that if her father were home, Spencer would never have dared to walk right into the house like this.

"There's plenty of milk," she told Spencer. "I'll put it on the porch, so Murphy can have some, too." Spencer meowed his approval. Ellen bent over the cedar box they used to keep the day's milk cool and safe from flies. She tipped the lid up, then lifted out the milk pail and set it up on the sideboard. Then, carrying the cats' cracked blue bowl, she glanced out the door into the night again.

Ellen walked out onto the porch and stood staring eastward, out over the pastures in the direction her grandfather had ridden. At that moment the moon peeked above the black horizon. She felt a little knot in her stomach loosen.

If Grampa could see, he would be all right. For all his age, his eyes and ears were better than most people's would ever be. Deerfoot was a good, solid, night horse. Grampa said she was as good as any he had ever ridden, and that was the best compliment a cowboy could pay a horse. If there was a stampede in the dark, a cowboy's life depended on the horse that could carry him headlong through the dust-choked blackness in a race with the thundering cattle—without faltering or falling.

As Ellen watched, the cream-colored dome of the moon rose higher, its circle swelling, filling out as it came up. Good. Now Grampa would be able to see—and so would Deerfoot.

A nudge at Ellen's leg reminded her what she had been about. She apologized to Spencer and hurried to pour the milk. The big gray and white tomcat purred his thanks as she set the bowl on the edge of the porch, as far away from the rectangle of lantern light spilling from the doorway as she could. Spencer leaned against her leg for a moment, staring up at her with amber eyes. Then he lowered his head and lapped at the milk.

"You are very welcome," Ellen told him. "But I had better get out of the way if Murphy is going to come up on the porch. You know she won't come within twenty feet if she can see me."

Spencer didn't look up from his lapping as Ellen turned to go back inside. The rhythm of his pink tongue seemed to blend into the rhythm of the crickets' chirping. Ellen wrinkled her brow, trying to recall if the crickets had sung as loudly the night before. They had been subdued all summer, their chirping muted and soft. Grampa said it was the lack of rain. But people blamed everything from arthritis to late babies on the drouth. They also spent the hot days and nights watching for signs that the weather was going to change—listening to crickets and roosters—and praying.

At the doorway Ellen hesitated. She looked back over her shoulder at the moon, then chided herself for worrying. Grampa had been taking care of cattle all of his life. He would be back in a few minutes. Whatever the problem was, they would manage somehow until her father came home the next evening.

Ellen left the door standing wide. She crossed to the hearth once more and stirred the coals with a slim iron rod her grandfather had won in a bet with the camp cook on a trail drive. One end was flattened and spread, the other looped. Ellen fit it back over its hook.

Sometimes Ellen hated living so far from a big town. They could afford a cookstove now—what they couldn't afford was the cost of shipping it from St. Louis to Dodge City, Kansas, then the wagon freight charges from there to Mobeetie. The best cookstoves were made of cast iron and they were *heavy*. But even sheet metal stoves weighed a lot. It would have cost as much to buy and ship an iron stove as it had to ship their two Eclipse Windmills—and that had set them back for nearly two years.

Ellen lifted the bucket and poured about half the water into the tin basin. Then she shifted the pot of beans to the rear of the hearth and set the water basin on the coals in front. The dishes had piled up since day before yesterday. It would take hot water to get them clean.

While she waited for the water to heat, Ellen peeked out the doorway. Murphy was drinking milk from the saucer. Spencer stood beside her, his tail twitching as he sniffed the night air. Murphy lifted her head every few seconds to peer out across the yard. The moonlight had edged the wilting weeds in blue silver. It lit Murphy's face just enough for Ellen to see the brown tabby markings that flared from the corners of her eyes and ran in lines across her forehead like worry wrinkles.

Ellen ducked back inside. She glanced at the hearth. The dishwater wasn't even steaming yet. Grampa was probably more than halfway to the east pasture gate by now. For a few seconds, her mind produced images of Deerfoot stumbling in a prairie dog hole, of her grandfather sprawled on the ground, hurt. But then she shook her head, impatient with herself.

Grampa was no fool. He would ride slowly unless he thought there was some kind of emergency. He had always said that men who took risks for no reason ought to be hanged for stupidity.

Ellen thought about writing more in her diary, and remembered that she had left it under the porch chair. She hesitated. If she went out, Murphy would streak for cover. She usually kept her diary hidden. She knew her father was curious about what she wrote. He probably wouldn't think twice about reading it if he found the diary lying about when she wasn't in the house. Grampa wouldn't, but then, even if he wanted to, he couldn't. He had never learned to read.

Ellen looked out the door again. Murphy saw her and leapt lightly off the porch. Spencer stared, disapproval clear on his broad face.

"I'm sorry," Ellen said quietly. Spencer twitched his tail and turned his back on her. Then he dropped off the edge of the porch to join Murphy in the dusty, moonlit yard.

Ellen went out and picked up her diary, then straightened, staring out at the night. She could see a row of faint, narrow gleams, arrow straight, leading off to the east. The ribbon wire caught the moonlight. From here it looked almost pretty. Up close, there were ugly barbs that jutted out both sides like steel thorns. It held their cattle in—and kept other people's out—but Ellen still hated it.

If any living thing got caught in the ribbon wire and struggled, the merciless metal would cut it to pieces. She and her father had found a deer once, an old stag that had tried to jump the fence and had ended up tangled in the wire. Her father had shot it, not because they had needed the meat, but because it had been hopelessly hurt.

Ellen heard the distant sound of cattle bawling off to the east. It was louder, more distinct. Her heart speeded a little. Maybe Grampa had ridden faster than she thought. The cattle were probably just bawling at the sight of a horse and man this late at night. They hated anything that broke their routine. Left to themselves they would travel the same paths, rub their withers on the same low branches, and graze the same meadows day after day, all their lives—unless something forced them to change.

"Like an old cowboy with a riata," Ellen said aloud. "With knees so bad he shouldn't be riding at all." She smiled. Grampa was probably just riding the pasture, checking the fenceline, the cattle. He would make his presence known to any wild predators that slid through the darkness. Barbed wire didn't even slow down wolves, or coyotes. But man-smell could, at least for a while.

As if to echo her thought, a distant pack of coyotes somewhere west of the house set up the wailing clatter that meant they were gathered to hunt. Ellen listened as the far-off yipping became higher and quicker, nearly frantic. It was an unearthly sound, but one she was used to.

If Ellen had been blindfolded, she would have known that the moon was full. It was on well-lit nights like this that the coyotes did their best hunting. Few rabbits or mice could withstand the urge to run from such maniacal noise. Once they left cover, the coyotes would chase them down by the light of the moon.

Ellen went back into the little house and lifted the blanket that set her bed apart from the rest of the room. She slid the diary beneath what Grampa called her soogans, a thick quilt her mother had made.

Ellen heard another cow lowing, this time from the big west pasture, back up behind the house. There weren't many cattle in it now, only a few her father had separated because they had been too thin to make the drive. He was trying to let the grass grow up there. But without rain, how could it?

Ellen fidgeted, smoothing her bed, knowing

that when she ducked out from beneath her privacy blankets, she would end up staring out the door again. The house seemed too quiet without anyone in it but herself.

"Keep busy," Ellen told herself. "You could walk down and see that Fay's all right."

But instead, she went back out into the main room and looked out the door at the silvered darkness. The dishwater was starting to steam a little—she would be able to clean up the supper mess soon. She stoked the fire.

Ellen straightened her father's blankets, then turned to Grampa's cot. He used his old cowboy bedroll on top of the cot's rope webbing—instead of a corn shuck and cotton rag mattress like hers and her father's. The long canvas bedroll was folded up, doubled so it just fit the cot. His soogans lay neatly folded at the foot end. The top quilt on the stack was one Ellen's mother had made as a girl. On a nail above the cot hung a dark leather holster. The ivory handle of a Colt six-shooter stuck out the top. Grampa used it only for snakes now, but he kept it clean and ready for use, just as he kept his long, braided riata and his saddle oiled.

A tinny hum came from the hearth. Ellen turned. The water in the basin was beginning to boil. She pulled it off the fire and poured half of it into a bucket for rinse water. Then she hoisted the tin basin up on the sideboard.

Ellen picked up the lump of brown soap and swished it around until a few bubbles appeared. Then she stacked the dirty dishes in the basin, letting them sink beneath the hot water.

The little can of scouring sand was on the shelf above the hearth. Ellen got it down and took a clean dishrag from the folded stack on the sideboard. The hot water and strong lye soap cut the sticky remains of their beans and corn bread quickly. She laid each clean dish on a muslin cloth spread over the sideboard, out of her way. She washed the frying pan last so that the beef tallow wouldn't stick to everything else.

Once everything was clean, Ellen lifted the basin again. Leaning back against the weight, walking slowly to keep the water from sloshing out, she went out on the porch and carefully poured the water onto the trumpet vine.

Just as Ellen swung back around with the empty basin, she heard a clopping sound that made her catch her breath, then let it out in relief. The knot in her stomach loosened and fell free. Good. Grampa was back. Now she could quit worrying. She stood and listened, expecting the hoofbeats to stop at the barn. But they kept coming. Ellen set down the basin and stood at the edge of the porch, nervously wiping her hands on her apron.

"Grampa?"

There was no answer. The dust-muffled clopping of Deerfoot's hooves came closer.

"Grampa?" Ellen yelled.

Deerfoot's hoofbeats went on, steady, and getting closer. Or maybe it wasn't Deerfoot? Ellen whirled around, astounded by her own carelessness. She ran across the dirt floor, grabbing Grampa's six-shooter from the holster that hung beside his bed. She turned to face the open door, her heart thudding as she waited. She heard a wind rising, sweeping the dry grass, rattling the windmill up in the west pasture. The hoofbeats came closer, slowly, as though the rider was hesitant about approaching at all.

Realizing that the lantern was bright enough to let any intruder see her long before she would be able to see him, Ellen darted across the room and blew it out. Then she ran out onto the porch. There, with the dark wall of the house at her back, hidden in the shadows of the trumpet vine, she stood, trembling, afraid to call out again.

As the muted hoofbeats got closer, Ellen raised the revolver, her thumb ready to pull back the hammer. She gripped her right wrist with her left hand to steady it, pressing her spine hard against the wall of the house. Whoever it was would not be able to see her.

She would call out a warning, of course. If it was a neighbor or someone who had lost his way and was looking for help, a drink of water and directions—fine. She would do what she could for him and hope that Grampa would not be gone much longer. But if the stranger meant harm . . .

As the horse came around the chicken coop, a silhouette in the moonlight, Ellen's hand began to shake. It was Deerfoot. But something was wrong. The mare stumbled, her head ducking suddenly as though she had stepped on her own reins. Ellen squinted into the murky yard. The saddle was empty.

CHAPTER FOUR

Ellen set the revolver on the rough cedar planks and ran down the porch steps. Deerfoot whickered, stopped, and lowered her head. Ellen picked up the reins and lifted them back over the mare's ears. A little clumsily, because the stirrups were too long for her, she got into Grampa's saddle and pulled Deerfoot around. "Where did you leave Grampa?" she demanded. "You never wander off when I drop your reins. What's the matter with you?" She touched her heels to Deerfoot's sides.

The mare responded as she always did, with willingness and spirit. She was pulling at the bit, fidgeting, ready to gallop down the path that ran down the house pasture fenceline, all the way to the east pasture gate. Ellen suddenly brought her to a prancing stop.

It had been wrong to leave the gun on the porch. Ellen leaned back in the saddle, standing awkwardly on her tiptoes in the too-long stirrups. She almost turned Deerfoot around, but then a sudden chorus of cattle bawling made her urge the mare forward instead.

As she rode, her thoughts spun. Most likely Deerfoot had just wandered off, pulling loose Grampa's quick looping of the reins over a fence post, and had headed for the barn. Grampa had been right; Deerfoot wasn't used to being awakened in the night to go riding out over the pastures.

Deerfoot loped easily, surefooted and steady. Ellen held her in, keeping her to a slow canter and following the fenceline path. There were no cattle in the pasture to spook, and Ellen knew this path as well as Deerfoot did. There was so little danger of Deerfoot stumbling that Ellen focused her attention eastward.

The moon was well clear of the horizon now, but still low in the sky. It was so bright that there were soft black shadows stretching from the fence posts.

Ellen felt a little clumsy and off-balance in her grandfather's saddle. She worked to keep her feet in the too-long stirrups. She didn't need them to steady herself in the saddle, but if she lost control of the heavy, tapadero-covered stirrups, they would flop into Deerfoot's sides and spook her.

Ellen knew her grandfather loved this saddle partly because he had won it in a poker game from a southeast Texas, brush country cowboy, and partly because it was unusual here in the Panhandle country. Tapaderos made sense in brush and thicket country—they were made to protect a cowboy's feet and lower legs. Up here on the plains, thickets and brush were a rarity. Saddles for Panhandle cowboys rarely had tapaderos on the stirrups.

The sudden appearance of a cow in the dark startled Ellen into reining Deerfoot in so sharply that the mare slid to a stop, her weight on her back haunches. Ellen shook her head, astonished. There shouldn't be any cattle in the house pasture at all. The road gate on the far side was standing open—it had been since her father had left.

Ellen stared. It was impossible to see the cow's markings in this light. It was grown, not a calf or a yearling. Ellen looked for a newborn calf in the shadows around the cow's legs and belly, but couldn't see one.

Ellen Elizabeth Hawkins   43

The barren cows that had not borne in winter or early spring this year had gone with her father to be sold in Dodge City. The rest had big, six-month-old calves now, except for a few young cows that had calved out of season—their babies were still small.

Deerfoot shook her head, pulling against the bit. Ellen released the pressure on the reins, patting her neck to apologize. Another cow loomed out of the darkness and passed close to the first one, swaying with a long stride as she headed toward the top of the house pasture. Ellen felt a tightness beginning in her stomach. What was wrong? What had happened to Grampa?

Ellen urged Deerfoot forward again, this time holding her back to a jog. Twice, cows ambled out of the dark, so close that Ellen had to rein in. They made unhappy sounds deep in their throats, the white rims around their eyes showing in the moonlight as they veered away.

At the bottom of the house pasture, Ellen followed the fenceline, turning right and working her way along the ribbon wire until she got to the east pasture gate. It was open, the loose post tipped over sideways so that the wire lay flat on the ground.

Ellen pulled Deerfoot to a halt and sat very still in the saddle. Several cows were picking their way over the fallen gate, heads down, walking nose to tail. Rather than startle them and chance a tangle with the ribbon wire, Ellen waited, barely breathing.

"Oh, God," Ellen whispered, gripping the saddle horn as the cows ambled past. "Please let Grampa be all right." She swung down and led Deerfoot forward, dropping the rein over a fence post near the gate. Trying to hurry, Ellen picked up the loose gatepost and pulled it backward, straightening the ribbon wire carefully. Then she ran to get Deerfoot.

Panhandle ranch gates were simple. Her father had built the fence right across the gate opening—except he tied the four strands of wire to a loose post on the far side instead of to the solid cedar corner post that secured the fenceline coming from the other direction. Then he had made twisted wire loops big enough to slide over both the loose post and the cedar post. With the wire loops in place, the gate looked almost like any other section of fence. Once they were taken off, the loose post could be dragged back, wire and all, to leave an opening.

Leading the mare through, into the east pasture, Ellen felt a sheen of sweat on her forehead. If Grampa had left this gate undone, when he knew good and well that the road gate was standing open, something was wrong. Ellen pulled the post across, fixing the wire loops to hold it shut, then whirled around and hurried to get Deerfoot.

"Grampa?" Ellen called out. She could hear the fear in her own voice.

In the moonlight, Ellen saw cattle walking toward her, headed for the gate. She stood still beside Deerfoot. Cattle were used to seeing people on horseback riding past, or driving them from one place to another. A person on foot was a strange and fearsome creature, especially at night, when the cattle weren't accustomed to seeing people at all.

The cows nosed at the wire of the now closed gate, turned around, and made their way downhill again. As they went past her a second time, Ellen saw her father's new bull, the young Hereford she and Grampa called Colonel Hereford. That was one good thing. Herefords were rare in Texas and valuable.

"Grampa?"

Ellen called into the dark, mounting. She turned Deerfoot so she could hear an answer if it came. But it did not. Ellen strained to listen. There was a breeze coming toward her across the plains, hissing its way through the grass and rattling the cottonwoods and locust trees in the creek bottom. A moment later it touched her face.

There was nothing to do but ride the whole pasture, looking for Grampa. And as much as she might want to hurry, she couldn't. Not without risking a stampede. In the dark, ribbon wire was especially dangerous—frightened cattle could easily blunder into it.

Ellen let Deerfoot pick her own way through the herd, slowly, carefully, heading toward the far end of the pasture where the windmill spun in the wind. Ellen could see the wooden tower faintly, the big X of the cross braces.

Ellen rode along the fenceline, alert for any sign of Grampa. She called him two or three more times, then stopped when the clatter of the windmill caught her attention.

The windmill was turning, as it should be. But it was turning too fast for the little gust of wind that had come through. Way too fast. For the mill to spin like this was dangerous. It could tear itself apart. Ellen ran her tongue over the painful crack in her lower lip. They had two windmills—this one and the one in the west pasture. In drouth weather like this, a broken mill could be a death sentence for at least some of the stock.

Ellen nudged Deerfoot into a jog, hoping none of the cattle would spook. Another breeze swept up out of the dry creek bottom, and the mill went faster still, clattering in the night.

"Grampa?"

Ellen said it almost quietly. She was afraid to shout now. As she got closer to the tank, there were more and more cattle around her. They all looked wary, their breath coming in quick bursts, their eyes rolling to watch her as she passed.

Ellen let Deerfoot speed up just a little, afraid to hurry, more afraid to slow down. Even if they could find the money to replace a broken mill, it might take months to get a new one sent from the Eclipse Company to Mobeetie. Even with the buffalo bone dealers freighting out almost constantly, the wagoners still charged high prices to bring anything in.

Ellen sat Deerfoot quietly, keeping her elbows in, her trembling hands still. The cattle on all sides of her lifted their heads as she passed. None of them was lying down. Something had startled them all into wakefulness—probably Grampa passing through them. Where was he? She wanted, more than anything, to meet him on the way, cursing his long, involved, cowboy curses, angry at Deerfoot for wandering off.

Ellen headed for the far corner of the pasture where the windmill tower stood. It looked like a misplaced tree in the moonlight; the timbers were cedar, freighted in just like the fence posts had been, a foreign presence here on the grassland.

Deerfoot pulled at the bit. Ellen could feel her own pulse and knew the mare was sensing her anxiety. It was all she could do to keep from urging Deerfoot into a gallop.

"Grampa?" Ellen called once more as she got closer to the stock tank.

The windmill was still spinning too fast for the light breeze. "Grampa?" Ellen squinted into the darkness, the feeling that something was terribly wrong prickling at her scalp. After a few seconds, she realized what it was. She couldn't see the surface of the water in the tank. And in this bright moonlight, she should have been able to.

The tanks were big, almost thirty feet across, and lined with sticky blue-gray clay. It had taken a month to dig this tank deep enough to hold water belly deep on a cow.

Ellen could remember riding with her father six miles to the clay bank, watching him shovel the heavy stuff until his face was red from effort. That clay was still where they had put it, lining the bottom and the sides of the earthen tank to keep the water from seeping out into the sandy soil.

Ellen leaned forward in the saddle, tightening the reins at the same time so that Deerfoot wouldn't take her weight shift as a sign to canter. There was no shine from the water. No reflection of moon or stars.

So the tank was empty, or nearly empty. The

cattle were bawling because they were thirsty. Ellen gritted her teeth. Other chores had kept her busy closer to the house and in the west pasture for two days. She should have discovered the problem and moved the cattle. This was her fault.

Deerfoot carried Ellen closer to the windmill, her hooves light and quiet against the earth. The mare knew cattle as well as Ellen did, knew how to move without frightening them.

The moon was a little higher now, and Ellen could see the blur of the mill blades, turning as she approached.

"Grampa?"

Ellen called out loudly this time, hoping that the sound of the mill had kept Grampa from hearing her other calls. Once again the seconds went past slowly. There was no answer.

Instinctively, Ellen scanned the pasture around the windmill, as far as the moonlight would let her see. She reined Deerfoot in, trying to stand in the stirrups, forgetting for a moment that this was not her saddle. The leathers were too long for her to raise herself more than an inch or so, and she could only manage that by straining. "Grampa?" Ellen heard the hard edge of fear in her own voice. Deerfoot shifted beneath her, tossing her head, pulling at the bit.

Ellen loosened the reins and let the mare go on, let her pick a path around the wide earthen tank. The dark mud at the bottom made the tank blacker than the night around it. Then, on the far side, close to the base of the tower, Ellen saw a shadow where no shadow should be.

Ellen stared at the dark place, holding her breath, guiding Deerfoot again. Not until she was less than twenty feet away could she make out the form of her grandfather lying on the ground.

CHAPTER FIVE

Ellen lifted her right foot over Deerfoot's neck and slid out of the saddle, dropping the reins. She hit the ground running, forgetting caution in her fear.

"Grampa? Oh, dear God. Grampa!" She bent over him, her hands moving in fluttering arcs, unsure what to do, afraid to touch him, terrified that he was dead. He was on his back, his arms out from his sides. His eyes were closed. He didn't move, didn't respond to her voice.

Ellen bent closer and nearly cried out in relief when she felt Grampa's breath on her cheek. He was alive. Shaking, she looked up at the windmill tower in the moonlight. It was almost thirty feet high. How far up had Grampa been when he had fallen?

Ellen stood, trying to think. The mill was whirling out of control and there was no water coming out of the pump. That meant that the sucker rod was probably broken. Without the resistance of the water's weight against the rod, the mill would spin like this—too fast—fast enough to break itself apart.

Ellen tried to see the tie-down wire. She couldn't, but what had happened was obvious. It had broken. So Grampa had climbed the tower to turn the mill out of the wind and had fallen.

Ellen's thoughts rattled past. This windmill provided half the water for the ranch. If it tore itself apart in the wind, they would never be able to replace it in time to save the cattle in this drouth. Ellen clenched her hands into fists. But she couldn't just leave Grampa where he was while she stopped the mill, could she?

Shaking with indecision, Ellen dropped to her knees beside her grandfather. She touched his shoulder, then gripped it, gently rocking him for a few seconds, praying he would move—open his eyes and speak to her. He did not rouse.

Ellen tipped her head back and looked at the windmill tower, wishing desperately that her father would somehow arrive, right now, and take over, start snapping out orders. He would want to stop the mill before anything else, she was pretty sure. But what if the cattle wandered back and stepped on Grampa; or if a rattlesnake or wolves . . . or what if she fell trying to tie the mill down and then Grampa was left out here to lie in the scorching sun when it came up?

Ellen shuddered, trying to shove thoughts of even more disasters aside. For the first time she noticed the rifle, propped against the base of the windmill tower where Grampa must have put it. She stared at it blankly.

Ellen knew what she had to do. But what should she do *first*? And *how*? She couldn't carry Grampa herself, and she couldn't hoist him up and lay him across his saddle. An idea formed in her mind, but still she stood, paralyzed by indecision.

Deerfoot whickered, and the familiar sound brought Ellen out of her thoughts. She turned on her heel and hurried to the mare, grabbing the rifle as she went. As she clambered into the too-long stirrup, then up into the saddle, she knew she was making a decision.

She was going to get Grampa to the house. That was the first thing. If the mill broke, it broke. If the cattle that had gotten through into the house pasture wandered far enough to find the open road gate at the top end, so be it. It was more important to get Grampa safe to his cot where he could rest without anything more happening to him.

Ellen gathered the reins and turned Deerfoot back toward the gate. This might not be the decision her father would make. But it was hers.

Ellen touched her heels to Deerfoot's sides and the mare sprang forward. Ellen eased her back to a jog and held her there, her neck arched, pulling at the bit, as they made their way through the cattle. Deerfoot knew cattle, knew she should not startle them, but the reins were acting like telegraph wires now, transmitting Ellen's urgency and fear for Grampa. The mare wanted to gallop.

When Ellen swung to the ground to open and close the gate, Deerfoot followed so closely on her heels that Ellen felt the mare's breath on her neck. Ellen knew Deerfoot could feel the tremor in her legs when she remounted.

Once she was back up, with the gate closed behind them, Ellen let the mare go a little faster. The cattle that had gotten into the house pasture had disappeared in the darkness, spreading out away from the fence. She hoped it wasn't too many, but there was no way to know.

Ellen bit her lip. Maybe she should ride up and

close the road gate before she took care of Grampa. But it might be a waste of time, too. The house pasture was big—nearly 350 acres—and the road gate was clear at the other end. The cattle weren't running, they would likely bed back down soon and never come close to the open gate at all. But if they did, there would be hell to pay.

Once out of the road gate, and across the narrow rutted road that ran past the ranch, the cattle would be in mostly unfenced country that ran for miles, north past the town of Mobeetie and Fort Elliot, and west to the three million acre XIT ranch on the Llano Estacado.

There were ranches scattered all over the eastern part of the Panhandle, of course, and quite a few up along the Canadian River—but it might take weeks before someone found their cattle. In drouth weather like this, with the springs and creeks dried up, the cattle might not last long enough for anyone to find them.

Ellen took one deep breath, then another. Twice she lifted her rein hand, almost turning Deerfoot toward the distant road gate. Then she lowered her hand and shook her head. No. She was not going to delay getting Grampa to the house by half an hour or more while she rode to the gate at a cautious jog, then came all the way back across to the house. If cattle got out, they wouldn't go far. It was only a few head, she was pretty sure. She would gather them up come dawn.

Ellen shifted the heavy rifle, resting the barrel across her lap. She was glad she had brought it this trip. Next time it would be impossible to manage.

Ellen counted the cattle she could see as she rode toward the house. There were at least eight head, but she couldn't see well enough to tell if they were steers or cows—and if they were cows, whether or not they had young calves with them. Most of the calves were big three hundred-pound seven-month-olds, born in February or March. But a few of the younger cows had newborns. A new calf separated from its mama was scared and hungry in no time.

Ellen clenched her fists, wishing she could send Deerfoot into a gallop. She should have done something to protect Grampa from the cattle. But what? She had no tools, no wire, no wood. She set her jaw and kept Deerfoot at a steady jog, covering the ground without scaring the cattle.

Ellen reined Deerfoot in by the chicken coop. Hurrying, urgent, Ellen jerked one of the board-stiff rawhides free of the nails that held it to the side of the shed. Then, leading Deerfoot at a trot, she ran for the house. Deerfoot snorted and threw her head up as Ellen tossed the reins over the porch rail and hurried up the steps, dragging the stiff cowhide along with her. She let it fall just inside the door, then went back for Grampa's rifle and riata, untying it from his saddle. It was longer than her own, and stronger.

Deerfoot stamped as the riata fell loose. Ellen slid it over her shoulder. The mare shifted a little, and Ellen took a few seconds to soothe her. It was important that she stay calm—in fact, everything depended on Deerfoot's patience and calmness. No other horse on the place would do what Ellen needed, what Grampa needed, without making a dangerous ruckus. She rubbed the mare's forehead once more, then patted her lightly. "You wait here, Deerfoot," she murmured. "I'll be right back."

As Ellen crossed the porch Spencer meowed at her. The milk saucer was empty. "Later," Ellen promised. Spencer followed her into the house. She stepped over him as he tried to rub on her leg. "Later for that, too. I have to help Grampa, Spencer." She pushed him firmly away. Insulted, he straightened his tail in irritated little twitches and stalked back out onto the porch.

It took Ellen a few seconds to find the little square match safe in its place on the shelf. She struck the first one too hard, and the head flared as it broke off the stick, then went out as it hit the dirt floor. She kept the second match alight and raised the lantern glass with trembling fingers. The wick was smoking again, but she would not take the time to trim it now. She turned it down slightly and groaned as the flame guttered for a second. But then it recaught, spreading across the arc of the wick.

Ellen set the lantern on the table and lifted the rifle onto the cow-horn rack. Then she went to the kitchen box. She brought the small paring knife back and knelt beside the hide. At the tail end, she pierced the hide twice with the knife, cutting X shapes about two feet apart. Hands clumsy with hurry, she doubled Grampa's riata, pushed the ends down through one cut, then back up through the other. She pulled the rawhide through the holes.

Fingers flying, Ellen tied an overhand knot in the riata above each hole to keep the riata from shifting. She frowned, tying the ends of the riata together to form a circle. She could hardly imagine a cruder harness, but it ought to work.

Ellen slid the paring knife into her back pocket and recoiled the riata, using a thin strip of cloth from the what-not box to tie the coil in place. Then she pulled an old blanket from the shelf above her father's cot and rolled it into a tight bundle she could tie onto the back of Grampa's saddle.

Last of all, Ellen picked up her own riata, shorter and slimmer than Grampa's, but still strong. He had braided it for her out of rawhide strips he cut himself and had given it to her two years before for Christmas.

Ellen leaned over to blow out the lantern, then thought better of it. She would not be gone too long, and it would be best if she didn't have to fumble in the dark when she got back with Grampa.

Leaving the door standing wide open and the lantern lit upon the table, Ellen went back out. Deerfoot stood still while Ellen tied the rolled blanket with the latigos behind the cantle where it would be out of her way. Then she tied her riata onto the saddle where Grampa's had been, using the pair of latigo straps on the right side of the high cantle. Most cowboys carried their ropes there, just to the right of the saddle horn, constant and close at hand.

Making one last trip inside, Ellen brought out the hide. She stood it up against the porch rail so that the end with Grampa's riata threaded through the thick leather was uppermost. The cloth strip held the coil in place; it swung gently from side to side without coming undone.

Once she was mounted, Ellen walked Deerfoot up to the hide, and let her whiffle the scent of it into her nostrils. Rawhide was not a foreign smell to Deerfoot. Everything on the ranch had rawhide ties, or a rawhide patch. They used pieces of rawhide for bags and boxes and for repairing everything.

But this wasn't a small strip of rawhide. It was a whole cowhide, big and stiff and clumsy. It would sail out away from Deerfoot's side as they went, then flop back down. That was enough to spook any horse, especially at night. And just because Deerfoot was accustomed to the rank smell of rawhide didn't mean she *liked* it.

"Whoa, Deerfoot," Ellen crooned, sliding her hand up the reins until she gripped them close to Deerfoot's neck. "It's just an old cowhide. Grampa needs us. Come on now. Be steady." She walked the mare in a tight circle and came up beside the hide again. "Let's just get on with this, now, Deerfoot," Ellen said in the same singsong voice. Her heart was thudding, but she tried hard not to let Deerfoot feel her anxiousness. It would only convince the mare that there was something to fear. Ellen walked her in one more circle.

"Here we are, Deerfoot. You just stand steady now. Whoa." As Ellen finished speaking, she leaned out and gripped the edge of the hide with her right hand. It was heavy and unbelievably awkward, but

Ellen Elizabeth Hawkins   61

she had to find a way to carry it. She dragged it closer, then shoved the edge of the stiff hide beneath her right arm and clamped her elbow against her side. Then she turned Deerfoot toward the path. The mare sidled, blowing an uneasy breath from her flared nostrils.

"Just walk steady, Deerfoot," Ellen pleaded. "Just walk on now. We have to get back to Grampa."

The distant bawling of a cow made Ellen take in a quick breath. One thing was sure: The faster they got back to Grampa, the better. She turned Deerfoot gently, skirting the yard and the chicken coop, careful that the unwieldy hide didn't hook on the corner of the coop or the shafts of the old buggy that sat off to one side of it.

As Deerfoot walked, light-hoofed and spooky, Ellen wished that she had carried the hide on her left instead of her right, where it was closest to the fenceline. If the hide caught on the ribbon wire, she would have to drop it, and that would scare Deerfoot and every cow in the pasture within earshot.

Ellen glanced in the direction of the road gate as she followed the fenceline, wondering once more if she should take the time to ride across the pasture to close it. It would have taken ten minutes in the daytime, at a gallop.

"But it isn't daytime, and you have to carry this"—She hitched the hide up higher under her arm as she talked to herself—"all the way to the east pasture without dropping it. Forget the gate for now. Keep your mind on Grampa."

Ellen settled into the saddle and tried to convince Deerfoot with her steady weight and posture that nothing was wrong. The mare was still pretty dancey—not exactly shying, but her neck was arched and her eyes rolled back every few seconds. She was trying to see the hide, to make sure it wasn't the live thing it acted like, scudding over the dirt where the ground was uneven, bouncing against her side.

After a time, Ellen tucked the reins under her thigh and reached across to adjust the hide. Deerfoot sidestepped and it struck the ground, and Ellen nearly lost her grip on it. She managed to shove it back just as Deerfoot stopped.

Ellen rocked forward in the saddle, then looked up, startled to see the east pasture gate in front of them. She reached out, lifting the hide, and leaned it precariously against the cedar corner post. She heard the wire creak as she released the hide, but it didn't fall or slide sideways.

Ellen got down from the saddle and put her shoulder against the loose gatepost, pushing until the wire loop that held it and the fence post together loosened. Using her thumbs to lift it off the corner post, she freed the gate and walked it backward, the wire dragging through the dust. She brought Deerfoot through first. Then she tied her to the fence inside the east pasture and ran back through the open gate to get the cowhide.

As Ellen wrestled it through the gate, she heard cows bawling again. They were thirsty. That was why they had found the open gate so quickly and wandered into the home pasture so boldly. They were looking for water and they could smell the full tank in the west pasture above the house.

Ellen grimaced, wishing again she had checked the tank earlier, had seen the problem in the daylight when she could have moved the cattle up to the west pasture.

Ellen propped the cow skin on the fence, tightening the cloth strip that held the coil of the riata together before she hurried to close the gate.

Deerfoot let her mount, then balked at approaching the rawhide. "Please, Deerfoot," Ellen begged, pressing her legs against the mare's sides and leaning forward. The mare raised her head abruptly, tossing her mane. Ellen turned her in a circle, then back, willing her to stop fooling around, to stand parallel to the fence, but she refused, sidling away from the rawhide. Every time the mare balked, Ellen brought her back around to try again.

Finally, Deerfoot relented and moved close enough for Ellen to grip the edge of the hide. As she tucked it under her arm she felt her already tired muscles clench painfully in the unnatural position. She ignored the discomfort and held the hide tightly against her side.

"Now, be good," Ellen said to the mare as she guided her into the pasture, heading for the windmill on the far side. "Be good and calm and remember how much you like Grampa. I don't have the strength to get him home alone." Ellen heard the fear in her own voice and cleared her throat.

Somewhere in the moonlight ahead of them a cow snorted, startled by the odd silhouette coming toward it. "It's all right, you fool cow," Ellen scolded in her best gruff voice, trying to sound like her father. "You know me and you know Deerfoot. And this old hide isn't going to hurt you a bit."

The cow snorted once more and leapt out of their way, but it stood its ground when they had passed it. Ellen glanced back to see it still watching them. A little farther on, a steer scrambled off, backing away stiff legged. Ellen turned Deerfoot to give the steer more room; it stopped and stood its ground, its head lowered.

Ellen pressed her aching arm harder against

her side, desperately trying to hold the hide up. If she dropped it, Deerfoot would spook, and the jumpy cattle *would* run.

When Ellen finally reached the windmill, she stopped Deerfoot a little ways from her grandfather. Slowly, carefully, she leaned out the saddle and lowered the hide almost to the ground before she allowed it to fall. Deerfoot shied a little as it hit, stirring up puffs of dust. Ellen dismounted and hurriedly led Deerfoot to the windmill tower. She tied the reins to one of the thick timbers, then whirled and ran to her grandfather.

When she knelt beside him and leaned close to peer into his face, she could hear him breathing, slow and deep. She had not realized how frightened she had been for him until tears of relief washed down her cheeks.

CHAPTER SIX

Ellen positioned the board-stiff hide as close to her grandfather's side as she could. "Dear God, don't let me hurt him worse by moving him," she prayed aloud. She ran her hands down his arms, straightening them close to his body. Then she shifted, straddling his feet, gently pulling his legs as straight as his crooked joints would allow.

Ellen took a deep breath and moved the coil of riata, laying it in the dust just above the hide, where it would be out of her way. Then she went back to work. Standing behind him, Ellen slid her hands as far beneath her grandfather's shoulders as she could. Gripping his shirt, she lifted him as well as she could, and dragged him sideways. His sleeve caught on the edge of the hide.

Ellen strained, managing to lift him a little higher. This time when she let Grampa's weight settle back onto it, his shoulders and torso were catercorner on the rawhide.

Breathing hard, Ellen positioned herself over Grampa's legs. Holding his feet, she started to pull the lower half of his body onto the hide, too. But just as she lifted him, he groaned and pulled one boot free of her grasp.

Ellen bent quickly, staring into Grampa's face. Was he coming to? He groaned again and turned, rolling back off the hide. Ellen cried out and reached for his hand. "Grampa, don't. Grampa?" He didn't answer, didn't open his eyes. He lay still again.

Heart beating fast, Ellen started over, easing him onto the hide once more, shoulders first, then his legs. He made a little grunting sound as she positioned him this time, but quieted again.

Ellen stood back, her knees unsteady. What would happen if he moved once she had Deerfoot hitched to the hide? Close to tears, she pushed her braid back over her shoulder. Deerfoot whickered, and Ellen spun around, startled. The mare had turned as far as her tied reins would allow and was standing attentively, her eyes shining in the moonlight, watching. The angular, crisscrossing shadow of the tower marked the mare's face and back. She flared her nostrils, and Ellen could hear her taking in long breaths. She scented something.

A coyote began to yip in the distance, and Ellen relaxed. It was quite a ways off. Then Ellen's eyes fell on the rolled blanket, tied by the latigos behind the saddle. She had thought to use it as a pillow for Grampa's head, but maybe it would work to keep him in place. She went to get it, glancing back once at Grampa's still form.

The slipknots in the latigos pulled free easily, and Ellen untied her riata, too, shouldering the coil of rawhide rope. She carried both back and knelt beside her grandfather.

It took a few minutes to fold the blanket so that she could tuck it tightly around her grandfather's body, working enough of it beneath him so that his own weight would keep him bound in the woolen cloth. Then she doubled her riata and laid it out on the ground, just above the hide.

Ellen glanced up. The moon was sailing high above the horizon now. It was small and white, and the stars around it glittered brightly—as bright as they had been all summer in the dry, clear air. A wisp of cloud shone in the light of the moon, and for a second, Ellen just stared at it. A cloud? She had not seen a cloud in months.

The wooden rattle of the mill had slowed, and Ellen looked up at it. The breeze had fallen. Ellen's spirits rose a little. Good. Maybe she would have time to do everything. Maybe. If she hurried.

Deerfoot let out a breath, whiffling it through her soft nostrils, and stamped a forefoot. Ellen straightened and faced her. "Now, you be good and we won't be long at all. Come on, Deerfoot." Ellen kept talking as she checked the cinches, tightening the front one a little. Then she untied the mare and led her close to the hide, backing her up very slowly until her rear hooves were only four or five feet from the hide. Ellen quickly checked the tied ends of Grampa's doubled riata together, then looped it around the saddle horn.

It made Ellen nervous to have Deerfoot's back hooves within a few feet of Grampa, but she couldn't think of another way to manage this. Still talking to Deerfoot, she led the mare forward, letting her pause when she felt the unfamiliar drag on the saddle. Ellen listened to the saddle creak, but knew that it had been made to bear the strain of a struggling cow. Compared to that, Grampa's weight was nothing.

Deerfoot took a tentative step forward. Her nostrils were flared wide, and her ears were turned sharply backward as she tried to understand what was behind her. The hide made a gravelly grinding sound sliding over the ground, and Deerfoot was nervous, her hind end angling to the left as she tried to turn and see what Ellen had hitched her to.

"Just walk straight, Deerfoot," Ellen said, singsonging the words, bringing the mare back around. "Just two more steps."

Deerfoot lifted her hooves gingerly as though she were walking on ground she didn't trust. She tossed her head.

"All right," Ellen said, "whoa up, now." She pulled the reins back, holding them close to the bit shanks, just beneath Deerfoot's jaw. "That's a good girl. What a clever horse you are."

Ellen stood patting Deerfoot for a few seconds, trying hard to calm her own voice, her own heart. This next part was critical, and it was all up to Deerfoot.

"There's nowhere to tie you," Ellen explained to the mare, rubbing her forehead and ears. "Nowhere at all. So when I drop the reins you have to stay put. No matter what. I'll be back before you know it. Whoa, Deerfoot," she added in a firm, low voice. "Whoa right here." She pulled on the bridle gently and leaned close. "Not a single step. Please."

Ellen dropped the reins and waited a few seconds more before she moved. She worked her way along Deerfoot's side, alert for any movement, any shift in the mare's weight that would foretell her shying, or worst of all, bolting. It would be safest to free Grampa's looped riata from the saddle horn, but if Ellen did that, she was afraid Deerfoot wouldn't stand still enough for her to reloop it.

Talking, one eye on Deerfoot, Ellen bent to pick up the end of her riata from the dirt where it poked out from beneath the hide. When she pulled up the other end of the riata, the rope fell across Grampa's thighs, not his chest as she had planned. She had led Deerfoot a step or so too far.

Heart thudding, moving as slowly and calmly as she could, Ellen worked the rope a little higher, pulling first at one side, then the other. Deerfoot rolled her eyes and stamped once, bringing Ellen around, her breath caught in fear. But the mare only stamped again, then seemed to calm down. Ellen exhaled.

"I need about two more minutes, Deerfoot," Ellen said in a low voice. "Two more minutes. You are going to get grain for a week for this. Not even Pa will mind after I tell him."

Deerfoot shifted her weight. Ellen hurried to bring the ends of her riata together, making a tight knot that held the braided rope across the blanket that covered Grampa's chest. Then she turned and took three quick steps to Deerfoot's side, one hand out to grab the reins. Once the bridle leather was in her hand, Ellen let out her breath.

For a few seconds, she stood still. Then she patted Deerfoot's neck. "All right. Now we just walk to the house. This part will be easy, Deerfoot. Just a walk." Ellen stood on the mare's left, her hand clamped on the reins just below Deerfoot's jaw. Slowly, steadily, she pulled the mare forward, one hand on the reins and the other on Deerfoot's neck.

Deerfoot startled at the first sand-hiss slide of the rawhide sled, but Ellen was ready for her and pulled her back, trying to settle her into a walk.

Most of the cows had moved away from them, but one or two remained, a little ways from the windmill. The nearest bawled at the sound of the sled and at the foreign presence of the two-headed, six-legged, drag-tailed creature that had suddenly appeared. It backed away, snorting, and Ellen held her breath, but she kept the mare moving.

"We don't have a choice, do we?" she asked Deerfoot. "I can't carry Grampa, and he can't stay out here until morning. Pa would have thought of something better, but it's just me tonight."

Ellen looked back at the rawhide sled. The white blanket looked gray-silver in the moonlight. Grampa lay still as stone, wrapped up like a baby and tied down with her riata. The dust roiled around the sled like smoke in the moonlight.

A heavy-breathed bawl from behind them

Ellen Elizabeth Hawkins   73

startled Ellen. Deerfoot skittered half a stride, but Ellen's full weight on the reins held her from bolting further. The rawhide sled was jerked forward, though, and Ellen leaned away from Deerfoot to look at it the instant the mare had settled back into a prancing walk.

Grampa seemed all right—or at least the riata had held and he was bound in place. As Ellen watched, his head lolled from one side to the other. Then he was still again.

Ellen looked ahead as far as she could see in the darkness, trying to guide Deerfoot away from the cattle, then back to see if Grampa had moved again. He hadn't, but Ellen was unsure if the first time had been because of Deerfoot's lunge, or if Grampa had started to come to his senses. If he did, if he started to groan or speak, she wasn't sure what Deerfoot would do.

A little bunch of cattle scattered as the rawhide sled came closer. They could almost tolerate a horse, even a girl on foot, but a man fastened to a stiffened cowhide was a mystery. They leapt back, hop-stepping and snorting, but none of them really ran. Ellen crossed her fingers, praying at the same time. They had made it this far. Maybe they would make it the rest of the way without anything bad happening.

"I'm just keeping an eye on Grampa," Ellen

said to Deerfoot, stepping a little ways away from the mare to look back. "He seems the same." She patted Deerfoot's neck and kept talking, telling her that they didn't have too much farther to go. The rawhide scraped over the ground, raising a ghostly plume of dust as they went. Deerfoot walked on steadily, stopping only when Ellen did, facing the gate.

"This is up to you, too," Ellen told the mare. "Just stand again, Deerfoot. Just whoa, right here. Until I get the gate open."

Ellen stepped away cautiously, glancing over at the ribbon-wire fenceline. It would be smarter to tie Deerfoot there—except that once she maneuvered the mare into the fenceline, she wasn't sure she could get her away from it without unhitching the rawhide sled and dragging it out of the way.

"This is the last big chance we have to take, Deerfoot," Ellen said, as much to herself as to her mare. "Get us through this one and we're almost home. The rest is just a walk up the house pasture hill to the yard. You know that. And most of the cattle are behind us."

Ellen kept talking as she dropped the reins and edged toward the gate. She had to turn her back to Deerfoot in order to slip the wire loop off the top post. The instant it was free she walked the gate backward, glancing over her shoulder.

Deerfoot was standing, but her head was up and half turned, her ears jutting forward in intense attention. Ellen shoved the gatepost away from herself, letting it fall as she hurried back, catching the reins in one hand and patting Deerfoot with the other.

"What? What do you hear?"

The mare's whole body was vibrating with tension. Ellen slapped her neck lightly to bring her head back around. "What is it? It can't be more important than getting Grampa home. Can it?" Ellen stood beside Deerfoot's head, pulling the mare forward with the motion of her own body, leaning into the reins so they could take the first step in unison. Deerfoot came along, but crabwise, craning back to face whatever she had heard.

"I don't care," Ellen told her. I don't care if it's a wolf or a rattlesnake or a black-tailed tornado. We just have to get Grampa home now."

Gradually, Deerfoot walked a straighter line and they passed through the gate. Ellen stopped a little way inside the house pasture and considered tying Deerfoot this time. But the problem remained the same. She would either have to tie her parallel—and therefore way too close—to the barbed ribbon wire, or lead her straight toward it to tie. And once she had angled the rawhide toward the fence, how could she straighten it out again? It wasn't a cart with wheels that she could back up when she needed to.

Ellen stood motionless for a full minute, trying to ease Deerfoot, to calm her enough to feel safe dropping the reins. But whatever the mare had heard had frightened her badly. She was still trembling and her head was high; she kept tossing her mane, trying to turn back.

Just then, Grampa made another low sound, rolling his head from one side to the other again. Deerfoot started. Ellen knew the mare well enough to know that her instincts were about to win out over her love for Ellen and the hundreds of hours they had spent working cattle together. If Deerfoot bolted, if she managed to get away from Ellen, she would hurt Grampa terribly.

Ellen clenched her fist around the reins, making a decision she knew her father would disapprove of. Any rancher would. In fact, even after she had decided, it went against every bone in her body to start walking—to leave the east pasture gate standing open behind her—but she felt she had no choice.

As she led Deerfoot on, the rawhide scraping along behind them, Ellen listened to two sounds with fear in her heart: her grandfather's low moans, and the nervous sound of cows' hooves as the herd, scared by the commotion and restless, discovered the gap in the fence and followed the scent of water.

CHAPTER SEVEN

Deerfoot pulled the rawhide sled slowly through the barnyard, around the chicken shed, and walked a wide arc with Ellen, coming into the foot of the porch steps. A little eddy of wind raced across the pasture and lifted Deerfoot's mane as Ellen stopped her and flipped the riata back, off the saddle horn.

Ellen led Deerfoot a little farther, then tied her to the porch rail, out of the way. Then she ran back to her grandfather. He had not made a sound for the last few minutes, and Ellen bent close to feel the reassuring tickle of his breath on her cheek.

As Ellen stood up, Spencer meowed from the

doorway. "Grampa's going to be fine," Ellen assured him. "He is going to be fine as soon as he can rest for a while."

Spencer meowed again, and Ellen glanced toward him. He was rubbing against the split saplings that formed the door frame, first his left side, then, with a quick about-face, his right side. He was anxious at all the fuss, Ellen realized, and trying to calm himself down.

"Me, too, Spencer," Ellen admitted. "I'm pretty scared. But it's going to be all right." As she spoke she stepped into the circle of the riata and positioned one hand on each line. "I am scared to death. But we aren't going to think about that now. There's too much to do." She looked at Spencer. "I left a gate open." Spencer paused in his pacing to meow at her again.

She gripped the riata tightly and took a step forward, leaning against the rope. The rawhide didn't move, and she pulled harder. She had to be strong enough. She just had to. She put all her strength against the riata.

The rawhide slid slowly forward and butted the bottom step. It was a low porch. There were only two steps. But to Ellen, afraid that the rawhide would skid sideways, the steps seemed an incredible height.

Ellen dropped the riata lines. Sitting on the top

step, bracing one foot on the side of the house, she bent to drag the rawhide forward, raising it inch by inch, until the top edge was just past the first step. She rested for a moment, catching her breath, then went back to work, standing up to use the riata again, straining to haul the rawhide up to the top step.

Breathing hard, but beginning to believe she could manage, Ellen leaned backward, her legs shaking with effort. At first, the sled would not budge, but after a few seconds, it slid forward a little—forward and up. Ellen closed her eyes and hauled at the riata, putting her whole weight into the effort, her whole will. The rawhide sled came forward again, almost a foot this time. Ellen rested a few seconds, then pulled again. Finally, the balance point was reached, and the rear end of the rawhide came up while the front dipped.

Grinning, relieved, Ellen heaved once more, a slow, steady effort. The hide scraped forward solidly onto the porch, carrying Grampa with it. Ellen let the lines go slack.

Dragging in one long breath after another, her palms stinging, she looked down at Grampa. He had not moved, had not made a sound since they had left the east pasture.

Spencer left the doorway to come closer. He padded toward Grampa, his nose wrinkled delicately at the smell of the rawhide. He meowed, looking up at Ellen.

"I have to get him inside somehow," Ellen said between breaths. She reached down to touch the top of Spencer's head. He butted against her hand, meowing again, then, before Ellen could stop him, he walked onto the sled. He rubbed his cheek along Grampa's leg and rolled half over, like a kitten wanting to play, his back against Grampa's work trousers.

Ellen reached out and scooped him up. "This isn't a time for you to play the fool, Spencer." He meowed, and she carried him to the edge of the porch and gently pushed him over. "I'll talk to you in a little while. You go find Murphy now. She misses you." Spencer disappeared into the dry weeds.

Ellen turned back to her grandfather. His cheeks were pale. But other than the lump on his head, he looked like he was asleep. She eyed the narrow doorway, then the rawhide—and she felt a wave of weakness go down her spine. Her makeshift sled would never fit through the doorway. What was she going to do now?

Ellen put her hands on her hips, trying to think. She had to get going, had to take care of the windmill, get the gates closed. Somewhere close by she heard a barn owl, three quick notes ascending a flute's scale. She turned automatically, checking the chicken coop for a lurking silhouette, then the moon-lit edge of the barn roof. There was nothing. She pushed her hands into her back pockets and felt the handle of the little knife she had carried with her.

"Of course," she whispered.

Whirling to go in the door, Ellen shuffled through the kitchen box until she found the skinning knife. Back out on the porch, working by the lantern light that spilled through the doorway, she knelt quickly and began cutting the hide as close as she could to Grampa's body.

The rawhide was tough and thick. The cutting took a while and Ellen was sweating in the warm night air by the time she had finished, but when she stood up, the rawhide had been trimmed by almost two thirds of its original width. It was narrow enough to fit through the door.

Ellen set the knife back on its shelf, then harnessed herself again and pulled her grandfather forward. After the first pull, she went around to the back of the hide to straighten the angle a little. Then she pulled it forward again. After four or five adjustments to get the hide turned squarely toward the door, she brought it through, onto the dirt floor of the house. Once more she stood back, taking long breaths, trying to figure out how she could get Grampa up onto his cot. Her eyes fell on his bedroll.

Ellen smiled. Grampa was so used to sleeping on the ground from his cowboy days that he preferred it. Quickly, she unrolled his canvas bedroll, refolding it to proper bed length, then laid it out on the far side of his cot. Then she arranged his soogans, folding each quilt separately and laying it on the bedroll. The last quilt she laid aside, across the foot of his cot. As warm as it was, she still wanted to have at least one cover on Grampa.

Taking up the riata lines one last time, Ellen dragged the rawhide sled closer, tugging at it until Grampa was lying as close to the bedroll as she could possibly get him. Then she carefully untied her rope and slipped the blanket from around him. She pulled off his boots and set them beneath his cot. Then she eased him onto the folded quilts, shoulders first, then his legs. He groaned twice, very softly, and his eyelids fluttered, but he did not open his eyes.

Ellen took his hat off, gently untangling the stampede string from his shirt buttons. She covered him carefully with the quilt she had laid on his cot, then stood straight, blinking back tears. He would be all right. He just had to be.

Spencer butted the back of her leg. "I told you to go find Murphy," she chided, still staring at her grandfather.

Ellen glanced around the room. The fire in the hearth was out—maybe there were a few coals beneath the white ash, but maybe not, too. She trimmed the wick, then lifted the lantern and swirled the fuel in the tank. There was enough for a few more hours. It would be better for Grampa to wake up in a light house than a dark one.

Ellen bit at her lip, picking Spencer up to stroke his broad back. He hung like a sack of wheat over her arm, his whole body limp with trust and affection.

In contrast, Ellen's thoughts were clipped, stern. Lantern lit. Fire out. Get the revolver and put it away. Hurry. Close the door on the way out. Hurry.

Grampa looked peaceful, comfortable. It was time to go. Now. Ellen did not want to leave him alone, but there was nothing she could do about it. She had to stop the windmill, and she had to gather in the cattle.

Ellen set Spencer down. She pulled her riata up from the floor by one end, coiling it, then slipped it over her shoulder. She got the revolver from the porch and put it away. Then she carried the rawhide back outside and stood it against the wall, her grandfather's riata still threaded through the holes she had cut, trailing across the porch. She pushed the rope out of the walkway with her foot and went back into the house. Then, with one last look at her grand-father, Ellen picked up Spencer and carried him out-side. He complained when she set him down.

"Can't be helped," she said to him. "I can't have you knocking over the lantern or nuzzling all over Grampa, and you would at least do that, Spencer, admit it. You wouldn't understand why he wasn't scratching your chest." She reached down to touch Spencer's nose as he looked up at her. "You keep Grampa company if he wakes up and lets you in, though, please?" Ellen heard a telltale rustle in the weeds and knew that Murphy was close by. "And you keep an eye on Spencer, Murphy." There was another whisper of movement in the dry leaves.

The moon was almost straight overhead as Ellen untied Deerfoot's reins. As she mounted, she thought about stopping at the barn to switch to her own saddle, but she rode past. There was no lantern in the barn, and it would take too long to go back and get one. Besides, she thought, touching the horn of Grampa's saddle, if she had to do any rop-ing, this saddle was heavier than her own, and rigged more strongly.

As they crossed the yard, Ellen heard Baxter cluck to his hens, his usually sharp voice soft with sleep. From the barn, Fay whinnied long and low. Ellen turned in the saddle to look back at the house. She could see the lantern light spilling from the little window.

"Nobody is getting any sleep tonight," Ellen told Deerfoot. "Not on this ranch." Ellen touched her heels to Deerfoot's sides, and the mare responded instantly, rising into an easy jog.

Ellen rode with her riata slung over her shoulder. She turned left past the chicken coop, swinging left, just wide enough to miss the old buggy, heading across the top of the pasture. The first thing she had to do was close the road gate.

Ellen passed three or four cows as she rode. They moved suspiciously aside to let Deerfoot jog by, but they weren't startled enough to run. Ellen was grateful for the moon. Without its light the cattle would have been far worse.

Once the road gate was closed, Ellen remounted and swung Deerfoot east, riding straight down the fenceline that bordered the road, feeling fresh, cool air against her face. The breeze she had noticed earlier was coming up a little harder now, straight up out of the dry creek bottom. She pushed Deerfoot a little faster. If the wind picked up, the windmill could shatter at any moment.

As she rode, Ellen heard a cow lowing outside the fence. How many had gotten out? She struck the saddle horn with a clenched fist. She had to get them all back in before her father came home. She could imagine the way he would look at her. He wouldn't talk at first. He'd be too angry. Then he would just look disappointed and sad, as if no one could expect better from a girl. Ellen hated that look worse than anything he could say.

The closer Ellen got to the east pasture, the fewer cattle she saw. She shook her head. Most of the herd were out, she was pretty sure. She should have figured out a way to tie Deerfoot for a few minutes without endangering Grampa. Her father would probably have some simple solution that she hadn't been able to think of—but what?

As she rode through the moonlit house pasture, the distant whirring of the windmill made its way into her thoughts. She could only pray that there wasn't already damage to the wooden blades.

Ellen opened the east pasture gate and led Deerfoot through. The windmill was easy to hear from here. As she worked the wire loop back over the pole, she felt a rush of wind on her face. It *was* rising.

Ellen dismounted at the foot of the tower and tied Deerfoot to one of the timbers. She looked up at the sky. The moon was a little past meridian now, a milky coin shining against the darkness. The shadows it cast were short; her own was gathered right at her feet.

Ellen Elizabeth Hawkins   87

Deliberately, Ellen slid her riata from her shoulder and recoiled it with quick, practiced motions. She walked around the heavy timbers to check the tie-down wire. If it hadn't been broken, Grampa would never have tried to climb up, but she had to be sure.

The wire was still wrapped around the spike nail that had been driven into the rough wood. But as soon as Ellen put her hand on it, she could feel it bend like a stem of grass, arcing over her head, back down toward the ground. Somewhere up above, it had rusted through. Ellen tried to recall the last time she had checked it. She couldn't.

Ellen pulled in a long breath and went back around to the ladder. The tie-down wire was attached to a metal bracket on the rudderlike tail of the mill itself. She would have to climb up and grab that bracket now and pull the mill around by hand.

Ellen glanced at Deerfoot before she started up. The mare was standing quietly, her head up, looking alertly in the opposite direction.

"You smell something again?" Ellen asked from the first rung. Deerfoot swung her head around at the sound of Ellen's voice. Her ears were pricked forward, but she seemed calm. Ellen started up the ladder.

CHAPTER EIGHT

Ellen paused on the third rung and gripped the ladder tightly. Her father had built it from peeled cottonwood branches, lashed together with rawhide. The branches were round and smooth—and a little slippery. Ellen could feel the vibration of the spinning blades through the wood.

She looked up. She had never climbed this ladder; her father had always forbidden her to play on the windmill towers, and he would never let her help with repairs. She wished now that she had disobeyed him at least once. The truth was, she had never really wanted to. She never climbed trees down in the creek bottom, either. She didn't like being up high like this.

"It's probably easier in the daylight," she said aloud, forcing herself to go up another rung. "Or maybe not. At least at night I can't see the ground too well."

Ellen looked up again. The ladder was nailed onto the underside of the platform her father had built at the top of the tower. It wasn't a very big platform, only about three feet across. And it sat just below the whirling windmill. There was a square hole cut in the platform—one just wide enough to accommodate a man's body—a slim man.

To stop the mill, Ellen would have to climb through that hole, then stand on the platform planks—with nothing between her and a twenty-five-foot drop.

Ellen thought about her grandfather and stopped, clinging to the ladder, fighting her fear. Had he fallen from the top? If he had, maybe he was more hurt than he looked, maybe he had broken bones and . . .

"Stop it," Ellen commanded herself. Her hands were shaking now, damp with sweat. "Think about what you have to do. Think about the cattle and Pa and the ranch."

Ellen climbed up three more rungs. A rush of

wind came across the fields. The mill spun crazily. The strands of hair that had escaped her heavy braid tickled at her forehead and neck. She freed one hand to push her hair back from her face. Her foot slipped a little on the peeled cottonwood. She slammed her hand back down, gripping the ladder rung, feeling her heart speed up. For a few seconds she just held on. Then she cleared her throat and took a deep breath.

"Just climb," Ellen said aloud.

But she didn't. She reached up and touched her cheek. When she had been nine, she had watched her father repair a windmill. He'd instructed her to stay clear, but then he had gone back to work and forgotten about her.

Intrigued by the clinking and tapping of his tools, Ellen had inched forward, without really meaning to, craning her neck to see better. The sun had made her eyes water, and it had been impossible to really watch what he was doing up on the platform. So, after a few minutes, Ellen's attention had drifted. She had begun playing a game in the grass at the foot of the tower.

When her father had shouted, she hadn't understood his warning but had only looked up at him, expecting a lecture. Instead, she had been struck in the face by the pliers he had dropped.

Ellen flinched involuntarily, remembering how much it had hurt. Her father had come down the ladder so fast, he had almost fallen. After he had assured himself that she was not badly injured, he had been furious with her. He had shouted at her; her place was in the house, learning to cook and sew.

But there was no one to teach her those things, and besides, Ellen didn't like working in the house all day long. She liked working the cattle. There was a tiny scar from the accident—Grampa always said he couldn't see it unless she pointed it out to him. But the cut had been deep, and the bruise on her cheekbone had turned purple, then green, before it had faded.

"If the mill shatters while you're just standing here scared on this ladder, Pa will never forgive you," Ellen told herself, looking down, then up. The moonlight silvered everything, made it pretty, even the rough cedar timbers of the tower.

She took a deep breath and made herself go up two more rungs, then two more. Then, she stopped counting and climbed, keeping her eyes on the platform. She stopped just beneath it, her knees quivering, unsteady. She gritted her teeth and simply hung on for a moment. Her arms were tired, and her hands ached with fatigue.

"Stop this nonsense and get the job done," she

lectured herself, hitching her riata higher on her shoulder. "You need to get back up to the house to make sure Grampa is all right."

Ellen swallowed painfully and realized that she had been breathing through her mouth. The dry air had parched her throat. She rubbed her tongue against her teeth, hard, so that she could swallow enough saliva to ease the painful dryness. All she wanted was for this night to be over, for morning to come and for everything to be all right. For a second she wished it, like a little girl would, with her eyes closed and her muscles tensed with effort. Then she willed herself to climb to the top rung, easing her head and shoulders through the hole in the platform.

"Keep going," Ellen told herself. But for a long moment she couldn't. The next step would take her off the top of the ladder. There would be nothing for her to grip, nothing to hang on to except the platform.

The mill was whirling off to her left. With every rise in the breeze it went faster. A clattering of the blades startled Ellen into moving one rung higher with her feet, which meant her hands were suddenly, terrifyingly, free. She tried not to think about the ground, about Grampa, about falling. She slid one foot out onto the platform, bending double to put the palms of her hands flat on the wood.

Ellen lowered herself to the planks on her hands and knees and froze. The vibration of the blades was almost unbearable through the rough wood. Her riata slid forward, and she shoved it back onto her shoulder.

"Now stand up," Ellen whispered to herself. She reached out to touch the edge of the platform, running her hands along the outside of the rough board. Behind her the blades spun in their endless rush. In front of her, past the edge, the night spread over the earth. She drew one foot underneath herself and rocked her weight back until she was squatting, her hands still on the planks for balance.

"Once it's done, you can get down," she reminded herself. "And Grampa needs looking after, and the cows." She waited for her knees to stop shaking, then realized that they weren't going to.

Pushing her fear aside, she stood up slowly, hands out for balance. She half turned, facing the windmill, feeling a weird pull that seemed to draw her backward, toward the edge. Once more, she positioned her riata higher on her shoulder.

It took all of her will, but she managed to take a short, shuffling step, easing herself to the rear of the mill. Slowly, trembling, she extended her hands, reaching for the iron bracket that framed the paddle-tail of the windmill. This close, she could see the broken tie-down wire dangling loose. As she grabbed the bracket, a racketing gust of wind came up. Her shirt rippled in the wind, and she held on to the windmill tail, bracing her feet. Once the wind was steady again, she began to pull.

Inching backward, Ellen brought the windmill slowly around on its pivot. Looking back over her shoulder as she pulled, she stepped carefully across the hole in the platform that she'd crawled through. As soon as the mill was sideways to the wind instead of facing it, the blades began to slow. Ellen walked it around a little farther, stepping backward.

"Now you tie it down," Ellen said, talking to herself sternly, as though preventing an argument. She heard Deerfoot nicker below, but she did not allow herself to stop or to look down. She pulled her riata off her arm and tied one end tightly to the bracket. Then she straightened. The hole in the platform was on the other side of the windmill now. She made her way slowly back to it, stooping to duck under the tail, her knees shaking.

Ellen let out her riata as she went, keeping just enough tension on it to stop a sudden swing of the tail. Then, making sure that the loops would fall free, not tangle, she threw the riata straight out and listened to it uncoil, slithering down the side of the

Ellen Elizabeth Hawkins   95

tower. The tail of the windmill, which usually kept it pointed straight into the wind, would keep it safely turned away—once she had it tied down.

Ellen sat down at the edge of the hole in the platform, scooting forward until she could get her feet on the second rung, then twisting to face the ladder as she lowered herself farther.

She felt the riata brush her back about halfway down and she reached out to take hold of it. She let the riata slide through her fingers as she went. The cottonwood rungs seemed small now, thin and fragile. It was such a joy to step down onto solid dirt at the bottom of the tower that Ellen had to blink back sudden tears.

Swiping at her eyes, Ellen walked around the timbers, careful to keep enough weight on the riata so that the windmill would not move itself back into the wind. She pulled steadily on it until she was sure the angle was right and that the mill was safe. Then she tied a hitch knot around the lowest of the timbers.

Deerfoot nickered again. This time, Ellen turned toward her. "It's done. We can go back up to the house now." Ellen's voice sounded strange in the sudden stillness. Without the rattling whir of the windmill, the night seemed too silent, empty. An immense weariness weighted Ellen's feet. She felt too tired to take another step. But she had to.

CHAPTER NINE

On the way back up to the house, Ellen tried hard to count cattle by the dull silver light of the moon. She had closed the east pasture gate, so no more would wander out—but she was pretty sure most of the herd was already out and gone.

By the time she got to the top of the house pasture and was rounding the chicken coop, Ellen had managed to spot only nine head of cattle, and not a single calf. Worst of all, she had not seen her father's Hereford bull.

"You'll be able to start riding them down soon," she told herself. The sky was lightening just a little. Dawn was coming. It wouldn't be long.

Fay whinnied again from the barn, and this time Deerfoot answered her. Baxter moved on his perch, annoyed this time, by the sound of the chopped-short crow he uttered. Dismounting in front of the house, Ellen was anxious. She could see the amber light of the lantern through the shuttered window, but nothing else. The rawhide sled still stood leaning against the wall.

Ellen eased open the door and went in, hoping to find Grampa sitting up, smiling at her. But he was still lying on his back, almost exactly as she had left him. His breathing was even and smooth, and his face calm. He had moved a little, because the quilt she had used to cover him was disarranged. His feet poked out from beneath it now.

Ellen pushed the door wide to let the acrid odor of the lantern clear out of the room. Then she went to kneel on the floor beside Grampa and bent forward to feel his breath on her cheek. Instead of reassuring her this time, it seemed to untie some knot in her feelings, loosening her control over herself.

Ellen touched her grandfather's cheek, her eyes burning. She refused to cry. It was pointless. She stared into Grampa's face. He looked perfectly normal now—not even pale. He would be all right. She was scaring the bejabbers out of herself for nothing. He had no wounds, there was no blood from his lips or ears. He even looked peaceful, like he was asleep, nothing more.

Ellen rocked back on her heels. An angry, grating meow made her jump aside. Spencer was twitching his tail, turning to lick it, giving her an angry look from the corner of his almond-shaped eyes. "If you would stay out from underfoot, it wouldn't happen," Ellen scolded him. Then she picked him up and pressed her face into his warm fur.

"I'm sorry, Spencer. You just startled me, that's all. I'm pretty jumpy. Colonel Hereford is gone. Along with most of the cattle." She let Spencer lick the tip of her nose. "Pa is never going to forgive me for that open gate. Maybe he shouldn't. I ought to have been able to figure out something. I was just so scared for Grampa. . . ."

Spencer meowed, interrupting her. He wriggled in her grasp and she set him down. He walked to the door and looked out, lifting his chin high and sniffing. Ellen stood up and went to stand behind him. "You and Deerfoot both seem to think there's perfume on the air tonight. I wish I could hear your thoughts." Just then the distant yip of a coyote pierced the night.

Spencer looked up at her, tipping his chin so

far back that she could see the white bib on his chest. He meowed again, insistent, urgent. Ellen bent to scratch his ears for a second. "Stay up around the house, Mister Spencer. That coyote sounded pretty close." Ellen straightened. She hated to leave her grandfather now, but she had to gather in the cattle. She looked at the sky. The moon was low in the west. "I'll have almost full light in less than an hour."

Ellen looked down at her grandfather. She would keep coming back to the house to see if he was all right. Even so, there might be hours between her visits. She shifted her weight from one foot to the other. Maybe she shouldn't leave him at all. Maybe she should be riding toward Mobeetie right now, to find help.

Grampa moved a little, and Ellen watched him intently. He did not groan; his face remained smooth, peaceful. Ellen walked to the lantern, making the decision once and for all. Grampa was all right. She couldn't risk losing the cattle—especially the Hereford bull. In a year as bad as this one, any loss was twice as serious as it would have been in a good year. The drouth had forced her father to stretch their finances as far as they would go. Any big setbacks now and they might not recover. Other ranchers had had to sell their places. Ellen knew her father loved this land. So did Grampa. She thought about her mother's grave, in a stand of shin oak on the hill above the house.

Shaking her gloomy thoughts away, Ellen blew out the lantern, then opened the shutters. The gray light of predawn came into the room. Spencer looked up at her and demanded her attention.

"I'll be back off and on, every few hours at least, to check on Grampa," Ellen assured him as she filled the canteen her father had carried in Mr. Lincoln's army. There was a dent in it from a glancing bullet. Spencer meowed again. Ellen smiled at him, speaking her thoughts aloud.

"I am going to put my saddle on Deerfoot. And I'll carry Grampa's riata in case I have to rope a calf."

Spencer made a sound of agreement and began to purr. Ellen lifted him up and rubbed her chin on his forehead. "You are always a friend to me, Mister Spencer," she told him as she set him down. Ellen corked the canteen and slung it over her shoulder. The sound of Baxter's first tentative, muffled crow out in the coop made her realize that it was nearly the hour when she usually rose to begin her day's work.

She took the milk pail down from its hook on the wall. Then she went out the door with Spencer close on her heels. She closed the door carefully behind herself. She untied the knots in her grandfather's riata and pulled it out of the rawhide slits. It was longer than her own, and a little heavier, but she thought she could use it if she had to.

"And you," Ellen said as she came down off the porch and turned toward Deerfoot. "You're my friend as well." Deerfoot lifted her head abruptly, and Ellen realized the horse had been dozing. She patted the mare's broad forehead. "I'm sorry, but there's still a lot of work to do."

Deerfoot shook, and Ellen stepped back to stay clear of the swinging stirrups and flying mane. Then Ellen stepped forward and untied the reins. "Let's go get my saddle and milk Dolly. By that time it will be light enough to go."

The milk pail in her left hand, her grandfather's coiled riata over her shoulder, Ellen led Deerfoot toward the barn. As they passed the chicken coop, Ellen heard another uncertain, half-melodic crow from inside. Baxter was warming up. She could imagine his furiously red face, his comb so tall that it folded over, like an off-center little hat. He would be more awake than his hens now, but later they would join him, clucking in the yard.

Ellen considered letting them out now, but decided not to. They had lost four hens over the past month or two. Ellen hated finding the sad little piles of feathers at the edge of the pastures where a coyote had made its supper.

Ellen glanced up at the sky. The darkness was lifting rapidly. It was probably close to five now. The sun would soon be a fierce gleam on the horizon. Then, in a half hour, the day would be sunny and warm. Two hours after that, it'd be hot.

At the barn door, Ellen unsaddled Deerfoot and let her take a long drink from the trough. Then she led her into a stall. "Eat breakfast," she admonished the mare as she poured a little corn into the feed trough. "But eat fast."

Ellen undid the throatlatch, then slipped the headstall of the bridle forward, over Deerfoot's ears. She eased the bit out of the mare's mouth. Deerfoot rubbed her jaw against the hayrick, then nosed at the corn in the manger.

Ellen hung the bridle on the stall gate and lugged Grampa's saddle back to the pickle barrel nailed to the wall. Her own saddle was just below it, straddling a small cracker barrel her father had gotten from the general store in Mobeetie. She tied Grampa's riata to the saddle, tightening the latigos carefully.

Then, hurrying, Ellen carried the pail to the second stall where Fay and Dolly stood side by side.

Ellen Elizabeth Hawkins   103

As Ellen came closer, Fay put her head over the rail, eager for attention. She was the friendliest animal on the whole place, except for Spencer, of course. Ellen liked her a lot, and Grampa loved her. Fay's granddam had been Grampa's favorite mount back in his cowboy days.

Ellen's hands flew as she milked Dolly, sending thick white streams of milk into the pail. Dolly grunted, offended at the hurry, but Ellen didn't slow down. Once the pail was full, Ellen poured in more corn, then went out of the stall. Fay nosed her way alongside and Dolly moved over, letting the mare share the feed.

On the way to the house, Ellen walked as fast as she could, holding the bucket away from her leg so that the splashed milk wouldn't soak her work trousers. Without pausing, she opened the door and went in to put the pail inside the box, taking out the old milk from yesterday. She would mix it with some corn for the pigs later.

Grampa had shifted again. Ellen straightened his quilt and touched his cheek, very gently. He did not stir. As she stood, she saw Spencer slink in the front door. She scooped him up and set him on the porch again as she went out, closing the door tightly.

"Milk later," she promised Spencer as she went down the steps and ran toward the barn. The sky was brightening fast. The cattle that had strayed would go farther and faster once they had daylight to travel by. They were all in poor condition. The last thing they needed was a long trek without water.

Ellen pulled a dry saddle blanket and her saddle off the barrel and went into Deerfoot's stall. The mare was surprised and made no secret of her reluctance to accept the saddle and bridle after such a small rest and feed. Ellen scolded her and reasoned with her and pleaded with her. After a few minutes Deerfoot stood still as Ellen gave the cinch one last pull.

Ellen swung up and rode Deerfoot out of the barn. She pushed the wide door closed without dismounting, leaning down out of her saddle to drop the bar into its bracket.

Ellen turned Deerfoot left and leaned forward a little, touching the mare with her heels. Deerfoot cantered easily across the house pasture, and Ellen felt her spirits rise. It was getting light out. The night was almost gone.

Ellen pulled Deerfoot up and slid off to open the road gate. There was a loose group of cattle standing a few hundred yards outside the gate. Ellen pulled the wire back out of the way, then laid the gatepost down in the grass. This would be the easiest bunch of strays all day long, she was sure.

As she put her foot in the stirrup and mounted, she looked out across the drying grass and counted. Six. Five cows and a big, mean-looking spotted steer that she recognized as a troublemaker. He would often lead a few cows off into a corner of whatever pasture they were in and try to avoid being moved with the rest.

The cattle watched warily as Ellen approached. The cow nearest her bawled pitifully, the cry of thirst that had become all too familiar over the past year. Ellen rode to the right, wide enough to prevent the cattle from starting away from her, close enough that they kept their heads up, watching. Once she was behind them, she gave Deerfoot her head. The little mare knew exactly what she was doing. She did not run at the cattle. She walked, her head up, alert.

"Heyup," Ellen called to the cows. "Come on now. On in. Heyup!"

The cattle stared, waiting until Deerfoot was uncomfortably close. Then they started off, staying together for the first few strides. A brindle cow veered off to the right. Deerfoot made a catlike shift to that side, angling just enough to start the cow back toward the others. She jogged then, closing the distance to the slowest animal in the group, the big spotted steer. Ellen sat still in her saddle, her body loose and relaxed, watching the cattle as her Grampa had taught her.

The brindle cow balked. Ellen called out again, slapping at her thigh with an open palm. Deerfoot changed her course and speeded up a little more, heading straight for the balky cow. The brindle's nerve held up for a few seconds more, but Deerfoot came on steadily and Ellen shouted again. The cow spun, snorting, to follow the others.

Ellen and Deerfoot worked the little bunch of cattle inside the road gate. Then Ellen turned Deerfoot to the right and drove them straight up the fenceline to the top of the house pasture, letting them stop not far from the west pasture gate. She reined Deerfoot in and took a wide circle around the cattle, coming around in front of them to open the gate.

The cattle stood uneasily in a loose knot. As Ellen walked the gate back, pulling the ribbon wire out of the way, she saw the spotted steer and the brindle cow start to drift, sidling off. The cow had longer horns than most; it was obvious she carried nearly pure Longhorn blood in her veins. So she was a little wilder, a little smarter.

Swinging back up, Ellen whirled Deerfoot to the right, cutting off the brindle cow. Ellen clicked her tongue, and Deerfoot moved them forward again, through the gate. Ellen watched as the brindle got a sudden wallop of water-scent from the windmill tank in the west pasture. She broke into a surprised, joyful trot. Bawling over and over, the brindle cow started up the gentle slope toward the stock tank. The others hesitated, then trotted after her.

Ellen closed the gate and walked back to Deerfoot. The mare looked less tired now than she had standing in her stall. Her head was high, her nostrils flared. Ellen realized that her own strength had come back as well. Maybe it was the ending of the long night. Whatever the cause, Ellen was grateful.

Catching a sudden sparkle on the horizon from the corner of her eye, Ellen turned to look. For a few seconds, she stared into the sunrise. Pink streaked across the endless sky, changing quickly into gold, then a pale blue.

Ellen knew her father would be well on his way home by now. He would have already cleared Palo Duro Canyon and been out onto the plains the day before. When he broke camp this morning, he would have been riding toward Saints' Roost. He'd cross the Prairie Dog Town Fork of the Red River by noon if nothing held him up. It would be an easy river crossing. All the water courses were low, or dried up completely. Riding steadily, he'd be home by suppertime.

Ellen put her right foot in the stirrup and reached up to get hold of the saddle horn. In one fluid motion she was back astride her mare. She put Deerfoot into an easy lope back toward the road gate.

Ellen found a second group of cattle less than a quarter mile from the ranch and drove them back. Then she located a third bunch and put them into the west pasture with the others. As she closed the gate, she could hear the cattle still stuck down in the waterless east pasture bawling. They were thirsty, too. The cows with young calves would have been the least likely to drift up through the east pasture gate. And if there were little calves down there, they'd get weak sooner than the adults.

Ellen pulled Deerfoot around, making a sudden decision. "Let's count what's here and then move the ones below up to the full tank before the sun gets too hot," Ellen told Deerfoot. "Then we'll go see if Grampa is awake." He had to be by then, she told herself. He would be fine, sitting up, wanting breakfast.

CHAPTER TEN

Deerfoot tossed her head as Ellen rode toward the east pasture. The windmill was still silent, safely tied down out of the wind. Ellen climbed down and opened the gate wide. She would leave it standing open this time. There was no danger now—the road gate was shut. So any cow that got out in front of her would just go up the path following the smell of water until the west pasture fence got in the way.

Ellen rode past the tank and windmill, all the way to the southeastern corner of the pasture. Where the creek came through in wetter years, there was only a dry gully, lined by chinaberry, locusts, and willows. Here and there a tall cottonwood spread its branches. The flow had dried up completely weeks before—but it had been low for a long time before that. The cottonwoods and locusts were still fine, but the chinaberry and the willows looked brittle and weary from the lack of easy surface water.

As Ellen rode, she kept her eyes moving. She worked her way across the width of the pasture once, then turned back and crossed it again, a little above her first pass, riding slowly, trying to check every clump of grass, every dust wallow.

Deerfoot knew this business as well as Ellen did, and when she saw a dun-colored cow that Ellen had missed, she veered enough to pass behind the animal, then turned, heading straight toward it. The cow crashed out of the willow and hackberry that had hidden it. Ellen patted Deerfoot's neck and kept an eye on the cow, so it wouldn't drift back.

Ellen carefully scoured the pasture, scaring up a dozen cattle, including two cows with small calves. But as she flushed them from the dry thickets and the rolls of land that hid them from sight, she was disappointed in how few there were. So many had gotten out. She did a quick calculation. Twenty-seven head were either out or still hidden.

"A few could be behind us," she said to Deerfoot as she drove the little herd into the house pasture. "But we can't have missed many. There're

Ellen Elizabeth Hawkins   111

more calves somewhere, too," Ellen added, speaking aloud a worry that had been at the back of her mind.

Cows driven by thirst and fear at night might wander away from their sleeping calves. The babies, listening to their instinct to lie still, would do exactly that, no matter what. Ellen had seen a calf crushed by a wagon wheel once—the little fellow had refused to move from his hiding place in the shallow, weed-choked ditch, even once it was clear the heavy wagon was coming right at him.

Ellen flinched at the memory, and Deerfoot flicked an ear backward. "Nothing," Ellen told her. "I just remembered the calves. There are seven little ones now, not counting the one in the barn. And there's the bull to think about."

Ellen felt her heart constrict. There was so much to do before her father got home. She had to have the cattle back in—especially Colonel Hereford. Ellen took a quick drink, never taking her eyes off the little band of cattle, then pushed the cork back in and tied the canteen onto her saddle.

At the west pasture gate, the cows smelled the water and were so willing to go in that she barely got the wire pulled back out of the way before they were starting through the opening. She left Deerfoot tied to the fence and walked behind the last cow, clapping her hands to hustle it through. She wasn't sure how long it had taken her to cover the east pasture, riding back and forth like that, but the sun seemed much higher in the sky than it should be.

"Let's go see Grampa," she said to Deerfoot as she stepped into her stirrup and swung up.

Ellen cantered Deerfoot up the path to the house, pulling her up as she came even with the chicken coop. She dismounted and led Deerfoot to the far side of the coop, and worked the latch open.

Indignant, his feathers fluffed, walking stiff legged and regal, Baxter emerged into the daylight.

"I'm sorry I'm so late," Ellen said as he led his hens into the weeds, clucking and scratching. He glared at her, then went about his business.

Ellen tied Deerfoot to the porch rail and rubbed one hand across her face. When she pushed the door open, Spencer came up out of the wilting trumpet vine and darted in before she could stop him. Ellen followed, her eyes too sunstruck to see inside for the first few seconds. As her vision began to clear she saw her grandfather, still lying on his back on his soogans, his eyes closed.

Her heart sank. "Dammitall," she whispered. And only then did she realize how much she had been hoping—*expecting*—to find her grandfather sitting up and acting normally when she came back.

Now she had to wonder whether she should leave him at all to hunt for the other cattle.

"But I have to," she said aloud as she knelt beside him. "Grampa, I have to go."

His eyelids jerked, and he shifted. Ellen held her breath. He didn't waken. His breathing was as deep and even as it had been earlier. She felt his forehead. He had no fever. Ellen picked up his hand and held it in both of her own. She smiled. Holding hands like this was something Grampa would never do if he were awake and alert. He often touched her, but the touches were fleeting, like the passage of a butterfly wing, a breeze.

"Grampa, wake up," Ellen pleaded.

But he did not waken.

After a few minutes, Ellen stood up again. She had to go look for cattle. She had to go look for the bull. Her father had pinned the future of the whole ranch on the Hereford, and the calves it would produce. It had taken a whole year's savings to buy the bull. Ellen hesitated. But what could she do for Grampa if she stayed? Watch him sleep?

Spencer was by the door when Ellen stood up. He meowed. "I can give you and Murphy a little milk before I go," Ellen said, suddenly needing a task she could manage without thought, without decision. "There's plenty from yesterday for the hogs."

Spencer arched his back and purred at her, loudly and gratefully. Ellen got the saucer and poured it full, then took it out on the porch. "You share it with Murphy, Spencer," she instructed him. Then she went back inside.

Grampa looked so peaceful, so everyday, perfectly *asleep*. Why wouldn't he wake up? She went and pulled his quilt down a little. She might not be back for hours. It would be baking hot by then, and even the sod-roofed house would be uncomfortably warm.

Ellen whirled abruptly and went out the door, closing it behind herself. She watered Deerfoot at the barn trough, took a quick look at the mama cow and calf, and checked Fay. Fay was lying down, but she got up and came to the rail to have her ears scratched.

"Don't let old Dolly bother you," Ellen told her. "And when Grampa comes down to check on you, tell him I am out looking for the dammitall Hereford bull."

Ellen found eight cows and a few steers down in the creek bottom just outside the east pasture fence. Three of the cows had new calves. The bunch was hard to round up and hold, and one of the cows finally slipped away into a willow thicket. Ellen drove the others clear of the creek bottom, then turned back to get the balky cow.

Deerfoot crashed into the willow thicket. Ellen

Ellen Elizabeth Hawkins   115

had untied Grampa's lariat and she swung it high, shouting. The cow stood still, ducking her head as though that would be enough to make her invisible. Deerfoot plunged toward her as Ellen kept up the yelling. She slapped at the cow's flank with the riata as soon as she was close enough. The cow finally wheeled and broke from the dry thicket with a great fanfare of snapping branches.

Ellen and Deerfoot followed, a little more slowly. Ellen raised her right arm to guard her eyes from the jabbing of a thousand twigs. Deerfoot lunged forward a second time, just as they cleared the brush, launching herself furiously at the retreating cow. Ellen scanned a half circle for the other cattle and reined in. Where had they gone?

Disappointed at not being allowed to chase the cow that had given her so much trouble, Deerfoot crow-hopped a little, coming down stiff legged enough to rattle Ellen's teeth as she stopped.

"Where are the others?" Ellen asked her. Deerfoot seemed to notice the absence of the other cows at that instant, and Ellen shook her head, tempted to laugh at the mare's sudden pause.

Ellen stared into the thickets in front of them, then turned around in her saddle to check in the opposite direction. The cattle had somehow drifted back and were behind her. She turned Deerfoot to show her, and the mare lunged into a gallop. Once she got close to the cows, she slowed, so that their uneasy trot kept them far enough ahead.

Without much guidance, Deerfoot gathered in the single balky cow, then pushed the whole bunch across the open country back to the ranch and moved them through the road gate.

Once they were inside the house pasture, Ellen turned to her right and forced the cattle into a trot, heading for the west pasture. She was acutely aware of every passing minute now. Her father was riding toward home at this very minute. Ellen put her heels to Deerfoot's sides and the cattle trotted faster in front of her. Then, suddenly, one of the little calves stumbled.

"Hold up, Deerfoot," Ellen said, pulling the mare back to a walk. "I'm crowding the babies too hard. Let's slow down."

Ellen shook her head, knowing what Grampa would say. It was always a mistake to make cattle run. Even fat, happy cattle should never be pushed—it only made them lose weight. Cattle that had been up all night and thirsty for two days were even more likely to be affected by human impatience.

At the west pasture gate, the cattle milled while Ellen opened up, then trotted through easily, as intoxicated as all the others had been with the odor of water in the clay-lined tank.

Ellen Elizabeth Hawkins   117

Ellen closed the gate, then rode for the house again. As Deerfoot jogged, Ellen recounted the cattle in her mind, adding the bunches she had brought to the west pasture together. She went over it all twice, to make sure. Then she sighed.

She still had eleven cattle to find, including Colonel Hereford—and two more calves. "Please let me find Pa's bull," she said, looking upward. "And the little calves, especially if they are separated from their mothers. They get so scared."

Ellen tied Deerfoot at the rail and clumped across the porch. She would straighten out Grampa's blanket and make sure he still had no fever. Then she would go again. As she put her hand on the door, she heard a soft scraping sound from inside the house.

"Ellen?" The sound of her grandfather's voice nearly lifted her off her feet.

CHAPTER ELEVEN

Ellen flung open the door. Grampa was standing beside his cot, one hand on the edge. His hair stuck up in spiky fans, the way it did in the morning before he wet it down and combed it.

"Grampa? Are you all right? I've been so scared, but I had to get the cattle back in and I . . ." Ellen trailed off when she saw how white his face was.

"I think I'll mend fine enough," he said, touching the back of his head. "I recall starting up that fool windmill tower. I don't seem to recollect much about how I got down." He rubbed the back of his head and winced.

"You should rest, Grampa," Ellen said quickly.

He nodded and sat on the edge of his cot. "I have a mighty bad head, Ellen. And my joints feel like a day in winter, all aches and bruises. By tomorrow or the next day I should be right again."

Ellen went over to the sideboard. Her hands fluttered like startled birds, and her heart was still quick and light in her chest. Grampa was bruised and hurt and felt terrible. But he was going to be all right. He *was*.

"Do you want some coffee? Or something to eat? I haven't brought in the eggs yet, but—"

"No, thank you kindly, Ellen," he interrupted her. "Tell me about the cattle."

She turned to face him, but couldn't find a way to begin telling him how long the night had been— how frightening.

Grampa passed one hand through his wiry hair. "I know I left the dammitall gate loose in my hurry. Did many get out?"

Ellen turned back to the sideboard. She ladled some water from the bucket into a coffee cup. "Yes, but I'm getting them all back into the west pasture. The tank up there is full enough." She faced him and, under the gentle pressure of his kind blue eyes, she suddenly started talking, telling him about everything that had happened, how scared she had been.

When she finished, Ellen remembered the cup

of water in her hand and crossed the room, extending it toward him.

Grampa held up a hand. "I don't feel like putting anything at all on my stomach just now." He had been sitting up. Now he laid back carefully, grimacing when his head touched the cot. Ellen set the cup down and crossed the room to get the quilt from her own bed. When she ducked back out from beneath the blanket that separated her bed from the room, he had closed his eyes.

"Grampa? I thought you might want this beneath your head." She folded the quilt.

He opened his eyes and smiled. "I would be grateful for a little softer headrest just now."

Ellen stood beside his cot. "Here." She waited for him to raise his head, then slid the soft quilt under carefully. He closed his eyes. Ellen fought the impulse to reach out and take his hand. He wouldn't stand for such coddling now that he was awake; of that she was sure.

"You go on out and see how many more cattle you can find," Grampa said without opening his eyes. "But you be careful. You keep your eyes peeled for trouble and if you see any coming, you just ride on back."

Ellen straightened. "I will."

"Promise me you won't take any chances."

"I promise."

"You think like a cow, you'll get them all. Including that bull."

"I hope so, Grampa." Ellen blinked, her eyes stinging again. She sniffled.

"Don't waste time on weeping, Ellen," Grampa said. "This is something you can still improve. Weep at funerals. Nothing else you *can* do there."

Ellen smiled. This was his usual lecture on crying. As long as there was still something to be done, he didn't believe in tears.

Ellen heard Spencer meow and looked up to see him coming in the door, his tail high, swinging like a flag in a parade. Without pausing he crossed the room and leaped up onto Grampa's cot. Grampa's eyes flew open at the sudden weight on his leg. Then he grinned.

"This spoiled critter will keep me company while you're gone. What time is it?"

Ellen shook her head and went to the door to look out at the sky. "After noon a little."

Grampa was pushing the happily purring Spencer off his chest. "You make sure you don't ride out more than a couple of hours from the place. Then you'll get back in plenty of time before dark."

Ellen nodded. "The missing cattle are probably still pretty close."

"Think like a cow, Ellen. They're thirsty."
Grampa grunted as he readjusted his position.
Spencer had lain down and now he rolled onto his
back. Grampa's hand covered his belly, fingers laced
around Spencer's paws. "Find that dammitall bull if
you can. Your father should be home tonight to help
if you can't. But try. By tomorrow maybe I can
help—"

"I'll find him. There's only eleven left out,
counting the bull. Maybe a couple of calves are still
where their mamas hid them in the east pasture."

"Open both pasture gates when you go out,
and close the road gate behind yourself. Maybe the
mama cows will go back for their own youngsters to
nurse them. Then they'll bring them back up to the
west pasture tank to be close to the water."

Ellen nodded again. She hadn't thought of
that. And maybe she wouldn't have. "I'd better go,
Grampa," Ellen said. "Do you want Spencer
inside?"

Grampa rocked his hand against Spencer's
belly. The big gray and white tomcat let his whole
body roll with the motion. Grampa closed his eyes
again. "Leave him be. I can use the company."

Ellen started out the door.

"Ellen?"

She stopped. "Yes?"

Ellen Elizabeth Hawkins   123

"You done a fine job. Stopping the mill. That was important. And getting my old carcass up here and in bed. I saw the rawhide out on the porch. That was smart. No one could have done finer."

Ellen smiled, even though he hadn't opened his eyes and couldn't see her. "Thanks, Grampa."

Clumping down the porch steps, Ellen looked up at the sky again. Her father could come home anytime between now and dark. All she wanted in the world was to have the bull safely in a pasture before she saw her father's tall paint gelding coming.

Riding out, Ellen opened the pasture gates. It felt funny, after all the work she had done, to get the cattle safely into the west pasture, but she knew that Grampa was right. They would stay right where they were now. They weren't likely to stray too far from water in the heat of the day. Only the cows with lost calves would be restless, working their way back down to the east pasture in search of their babies.

Deerfoot stood quietly while Ellen opened the road gate, then again while she closed it behind them. Once they were outside, Ellen checked her saddle cinch. It had loosened a little. She tightened it and then remounted. She recoiled Grampa's riata and tied the latigo with a slipknot so that she could release it quickly if she needed to. Then she turned

Deerfoot toward the open country.

She found six cows standing in a dry draw about three miles out. Bringing them back, she spotted dark shapes moving through some cottonwoods. Deerfoot veered toward the second bunch and Ellen let her go, hoping wildly that this group would include the bull. But as they got close, Ellen standing in the stirrups to see better, she let out a disappointed breath. There were only two rangy steers and a young cow.

Ellen turned them all toward home, setting a faster pace than she knew was wise. Once she had them safely trotting toward the west pasture, she went back out and closed the road gate once more. Now there were two cattle missing. Her father's bull, and one cow.

Ellen stood in the stirrups, stretching her legs and trying to decide where to look first. "Think like a cow," she said aloud, reminding herself of Grampa's advice. She had already ridden the dry creek bottoms and the open country closest to the ranch. Maybe the Hereford bull had struck out overland. Maybe he remembered the Goodnight ranch where he had been born. Grampa had told her that longhorns would set off for an old familiar range if they got loose before they were settled into a new home. But Herefords were much less wild.

And the JA was southwest across a lot of dry country—the country her father would be crossing on his way home.

The idea of running into her father and having to explain what she was doing made Ellen wince. But she was pretty sure the bull would not have gone that far into dry land anyway. It was far more likely that he had started off north, or southeast—either direction would eventually bring him to creek bottoms, and even though most of them were dry now, there would be shade and the lingering scent of water.

"Maybe we ought to ride north for a couple hours, or even all the way to the Sweetwater up around Mobeetie. We could come back in a loop, cover different country riding home." Ellen sat still after she said it, trying to decide. It was like rolling dice, relying on chance, and she hated the feeling. Still, what else could she do? One thing was certain: She would never find the bull by sitting here wondering which way to go.

Deerfoot needed only the touch of Ellen's heels to start forward, swinging into her easy, ground-covering jog. Ellen rode straight out from the road gate, going north. She kept her eyes moving, running her gaze across the country like Grampa always did.

But then, about a mile north of the ranch, she

reined in. She pushed her braid back over her shoulder and patted Deerfoot's neck. "I wish I knew we were going the right direction."

Without Deerfoot's hoofbeats to hold it back, the silence of the plains gathered around Ellen. A breeze came through the grass, cooling her sweat-damp forehead and neck. She stood up in the stirrups and stretched, staring into the distance.

She had already searched the creek bottoms closest to the ranch. If Colonel Hereford hadn't gone there, where would he be? He would have been thirsty, just like the rest, and the smell of water should have drawn him to one place or the other.

Ellen turned almost all the way around in her saddle, looking off toward the horizon, trying to think. She had to outsmart this bull. Maybe the missing cow was with him, maybe not. The bull wouldn't hesitate to take off alone. In fact, left alone, wild longhorn bulls often lived by themselves for months at a time.

Ellen sat back down in her saddle. The heat of the sun was like a weight on her shoulders. She looked up to gauge the time. "Nearly three," she said aloud. "He has been thirsty and hot all day long. Where would he go?"

Ellen urged Deerfoot forward again, this time riding in a long arc at a slow walk, scanning the ground for hoofprints. Maybe if she could spot tracks, she could at least figure out what direction the bull had gone. He was alone, or with one cow, and she ought to be able to identify the tracks if she crossed them. All the others had been in bigger bands.

After a little more than half an hour, Ellen was ready to give up on tracking the bull. Dozens of tracks crisscrossed the ground. Her father had passed this way, too, more or less, heading out for the JA four days before. The weather was so dry, and the soil so powdery, that none of the tracks looked crisp or new. They were all blurred.

Ellen rode on northward for another half mile before she pulled Deerfoot to a stop. She stood in her stirrups again, more to stretch her legs than to try to see a little farther. The truth was that there was just too much ground to cover, too many places the bull might have gone. Ellen wiped at her face with her shirtsleeve. The sun was still high, the air furnace-hot.

Ellen felt her eyes stinging from the bright heat of the sun. It was impossible to find a stray in a few hours out here in the open country. Besides, the creek bottoms close to the ranch were the logical place for a thirsty bull. She could have overlooked him in the east pasture, or later, when she had gone through the bottoms outside the ranch.

There were enough thickets and fallen limbs to make cover for a big animal.

Ellen almost started back, but then she hesitated. She had been so careful. She had doubled back a dozen times, making sure that she had crossed every foot of ground at least once, sometimes twice. It was hard to believe that the bull had managed to hide from her the whole morning.

Ellen impulsively turned Deerfoot southeast, riding at an angle that would carry her back to the ranch fenceline above the road gate. Suddenly her thoughts focused on a single idea: the fenceline. Ellen reined Deerfoot in. The mare tossed her head and stamped a forefoot in annoyance. Ellen loosened the reins.

"Deerfoot? This bull is a Hereford, not a wild Texas longhorn like we're used to. What if it is used to being in a fence and a little scared of the open? What if it just poked along the fence outside the road gate, smelling for water?" She pushed Deerfoot into a lope, wishing she could go faster. But it was hot, and Deerfoot had been working without rest for far too long already. Ellen wiped her sleeve across her face again. Then she crossed her fingers and whispered a prayer.

CHAPTER TWELVE

Once she was in sight of the ranch, Ellen turned Deerfoot westward. She rode the long fenceline, following the ribbon wire all the way to the northwest corner of the ranch. There was no bull in sight, nor the missing cow. Ellen wiped at her forehead and reined Deerfoot in at the corner post. She slumped in her saddle, discouraged. It had seemed so logical, so *possible*, that the bull would have stayed close to the fenceline.

Ellen blinked, covering her sun-weary eyes for a second with one hand. Then she opened them. The barbed wire went on to the south, bordering the high end of the rolling west pasture. Ellen sat still for a full minute. She could see the distant windmill, and the cattle dotted around it on the top of the slope that led back down to the house. It was almost a mile away. She brought her eyes back to the fenceline that stretched away in front of her. A flicker of motion caught her attention.

Ellen raised one hand to shade her eyes. She had seen something, she was sure of it. Whatever it had been, it had topped a rise, then gone over, moving out of sight before her mind could make sense out of it. It had been too big to be a bull, hadn't it? Maybe she had glimpsed the cow and the bull together, walking side by side.

Ellen urged Deerfoot into a jog. The mare was tired, Ellen could feel it. To waste her strength now could be a terrible mistake. Still, Ellen was afraid to lose her only chance to get the bull back by going too slow. She held Deerfoot steady as they started up the first gradual rise. As they neared the top, Ellen clenched her hand on the reins, hoping, pulling Deerfoot in just as they reached the top.

Ellen scanned the empty prairie, following the fenceline with her eyes, then sweeping her gaze farther out. She squinted to judge the distance to the next rise. It was possible that the bull had seen her and speeded up a little. If that had happened, he

Ellen Elizabeth Hawkins   131

could have made it over the next rise before she was able to see him.

Deerfoot was breathing hard. The heat was oppressive. This was the kind of weather Grampa always said was hard just to stay alive in. Ellen nudged Deerfoot into a walk. The bull wouldn't keep up much of a pace, either, she was sure.

Ellen rode toward the next wrinkle in the land, a brushy strip that she knew marked the end of their place. The next ranch wasn't fenced on this side yet, but it soon would be, her father had said. Ellen wished the neighbors had gotten around to fencing sooner. She would have welcomed another line of posts and ribbon wire to stop Colonel Hereford's progress.

Deerfoot jogged up the next slope, and once more Ellen reined her in at the top, staring into the distance expectantly. There. On top of the next rise, moving along the fence, were two dark shapes.

Ellen let out a whoosh of breath and dropped the reins to raise both fists in the air. Then she leaned down to hug Deerfoot's sweaty neck. "We found him! And the cow's with him, Deerfoot." As she straightened, she noticed that her saddle felt a little loose. She would stop and tighten her cinch again—but not yet.

Deerfoot cantered down the slope. Ellen held

her to a slow lope and pulled her to a jog when they started uphill again. If the cattle spotted her coming toward them too fast, they might run.

"And it's too hot for that," Ellen said aloud, standing in the stirrups to see as they came up over the rise.

The bull had stopped. He and the cow stood side by side, their necks stretched wistfully over the ribbon wire. They could still smell the water, as they had been able to all day, but were helpless to figure out how to get inside the fence to the tank.

Ellen rode up quietly. The cow looked exhausted. The bull was not in much better shape. Swinging wide, Ellen went around the cattle, then turned back toward them. Deerfoot held her head high, but her breathing was harsh and dry.

"We all need to get home as quick as we can," Ellen said in a calm voice. "Heyup, now. Let's go."

The bull was reluctant to move, but after a moment he lifted his head and turned, nearly scraping the wire with his chin. The cow was warier, her wide horns lowered at Deerfoot for an instant as she stood, blowing loud breaths out through her nostrils.

"Heyup." Ellen untied Grampa's riata and slapped the coil against her leg. The bull moved away from her, walking down the fenceline. The cow lowered her head once more, hooking downward with her left horn. Then she gave in and followed the bull. They walked, heavy hoofed, raising their heads and looking back over their shoulders.

"We got him, we got him," Ellen sang to Deerfoot. The mare was still breathing hard. Her coat was dark with sweat. Ellen patted her joyously as they went along slowly, the sun glazing the countryside with a yellow, honeyed light that made everything look gilded. The bull walked docilely, snorting a little only when the long horns of the cow brushed his shoulder. They plodded into a stand of stunted shin oak, the trunks twisted and bent.

At the corner of the fence, Ellen swung Deerfoot wide, shifting so that the cattle were forced to turn a little at a time, making their way through the shin oaks to start back down the long fence toward the road gate. Ellen was relaxed in the saddle, smiling. Everything was going to turn out all right.

A breeze came over the open country, and Ellen felt it cool her face. The fierce sunlight dimmed a little and she looked up, startled. High, wispy clouds had appeared in the sky, flying in formation, like ephemeral geese so high overhead that Ellen had to shade her eyes and squint to see them.

A sudden, startling growl jerked Ellen's eyes

back to the cattle. The bull was lunging forward, his massive haunches twisted as he heaved himself upward—the earth seeming to cave in beneath him. A shin oak tilted, swinging loosely toward the ground. Suddenly Ellen saw a coyote snarling, biting at the bull's heels. The cow had turned, wheeling around to break out of the shin oaks, toward the open country. The bull kicked madly at the coyote, twisting hard to run heavily after the cow.

Ellen held Deerfoot back, too stunned to react. The coyote turned to face them, growling low and menacingly at Deerfoot, then it noticed her rider. The animal stopped to stare, then whirled back into the brush. Ellen heard the yipping of coyote pups. It was only then that she understood what had happened.

The bull had blundered onto the coyote's den. The collapsing roof had brought the mother raging to the surface. This was probably the coyote that had been killing hens, the one that had been slinking close to the house where Deerfoot and Spencer could scent her.

Ellen turned Deerfoot, glancing back to make sure that the coyote had given up the fight. Then she leaned forward, pushing Deerfoot into a canter.

The bull and the cow were running close together. Their sides were heaving, and their shoulders were wet with sweat. They had a long lead, and Deerfoot labored to overtake them, galloping hard. Ellen leaned forward over the mare's neck as she pounded over the hard, dry dirt.

Deerfoot was straining. Ellen could feel the effort in every stride. Yet, inch by inch the mare gained ground. The land dropped, and Ellen sat back a little, keeping her weight balanced. By the time the land began to rise again, Deerfoot's muzzle was even with the cow's rump. A dozen strides up the incline and the long horns were dangerously close.

Deerfoot was putting her whole heart into the race, but Ellen knew she couldn't keep it up much longer. And if the mare faltered, Ellen knew she was going to lose the bull.

Ellen looped the reins around the saddle horn and used both hands to shake the loop in the riata down through the leatherbound honda, making it bigger and bigger. She had never roped a bull before. She had never even roped a full-grown cow. In fact, she had mostly roped fence posts under Grampa's instruction, when her father wasn't looking. She wished desperately that her grandfather were here in her place. He could rope anything.

Trying to remember everything her grandfather had ever told her, Ellen worked the loop a little bigger, then shifted the coiled riata to her left hand, spinning the loop once or twice with her right to warn Deerfoot of what she was about to do. The cow was between Ellen and the bull, but she was pretty sure, as close as Deerfoot was keeping her, that she could manage to get in front of her.

Ellen looked ahead again. They were coming up on a dry creek bottom, studded with cotton-woods and locusts. Ellen knew she would have to try now. If the bull made it into that kind of cover, she might not be able to get a rope on him before Deerfoot's strength gave out.

Swinging a practice loop one more time, Ellen leaned forward hard, and Deerfoot responded with a little burst of speed. The bull went on, and Deerfoot gave chase.

Ellen whirled the riata in three quick circles over her head, then stood in her stirrups and let it sail out toward the running bull.

The rope dropped neatly over the bull's head, and Deerfoot threw her weight against the rope so quickly that Ellen barely had time to dally the riata around her saddle horn. The bull jerked around like an enormous fish on a hook. The cow ran on, bawling when the taut rope scraped her back.

Deerfoot, sides heaving and eyes rimmed in white, plunged to a stop, keeping her front legs directly toward the bull. He slammed against the rope, his enormous weight dragging Deerfoot sideways in little jerks as she fought to hold her ground.

The riata was strung as taut as fence wire, cutting into Ellen's thigh. She had the reins in her hand again, and she tried to turn Deerfoot a little to ease the rope off her leg, but the mare fought against the bit, determined to bring the bull to a stop like any good roping horse would.

"You can't do it that way," Ellen yelled.

The bull shook his head, jerking backward, his whole body shaking with fury. The cow had stopped and was watching, bawling her misery to the endless plains. Over her racket, and the sound of the grunting, infuriated bull, Ellen heard something else. It was a rending sound, a series of sharp pops, timed to match an odd unbalanced feeling that it took Ellen a split second to understand.

The saddle was loosening. It had been loosening all afternoon because her cinch was about to break. Ellen looked down at the rope, tight as a guitar string, quivering under the tug of war between the bull and Deerfoot.

Lashing furiously at Deerfoot's rump with the ends of the riata, pounding her heels into the mare's sides, Ellen whooped, screaming at Deerfoot to move toward the bull, to release the tension on the rope—and the pressure on the cinch.

Startled beyond reason or training, Deerfoot leapt forward, and the bull was suddenly able to turn and run again, heading for the cover of the trees a few hundred yards away. Responding to Ellen's screams and whoops, Deerfoot thundered behind him, keeping the rope slack. Ellen freed her feet from her stirrups and sat the saddle fearfully, terrified that it would start to slide, turning to fall beneath the mare's driving hooves. Ellen stared at the cottonwoods in the creek bottom, willing the cinch to hold for another few seconds.

The bull ran crabwise at first, then he straightened, gaining momentum. His flanks were flecked with white, lathery sweat, and his huge bulk seemed to shake the earth with every stride. Deerfoot ran heavily, keeping up, her breathing almost a sobbing sound now.

Desperate, Ellen finally saw a stout cottonwood the bull would come close enough to as he ran into the creek bottom. She set herself in the uneasy saddle, waiting until the last moment to pull Deerfoot aside, veering so that the mare would pass the tree on the opposite side. An instant later, Ellen dragged back on the reins, slipping out of the saddle as Deerfoot began to plunge to a halt. The riata in both hands, Ellen hit the ground running. She was almost all the way around the tree when the bull's weight hit the rope. The riata sprang taut, and held.

Careful not to trap herself in the rope, Ellen sprinted around the tree a second time, wrapping the riata tightly, ducking beneath it on the far side where she came within a few feet of the furious bull. He stopped fighting the rope to bellow at her, then stood, stamping one forehoof, then another, shaking his huge head in fury.

Ellen leaned against the rough trunk, her breath heaving. There was no sound at all now, except for the pounding of her heart and the labored breathing of every creature around her.

Ellen began to giggle. Her hands were shaking, and her legs refused to hold her upright. She struggled to tie off the rope and finally managed it, wobbling toward Deerfoot. The mare was standing with her head lowered, her breath stirring the dust at her feet. Ellen patted her, leaning against her side, crying a little, then giggling again. She shivered. She was so soaked with sweat that the breeze made her chilly. Deerfoot stood spraddle legged for a time, then raised her head.

Ellen looked up, a sharp, almost metallic odor filling her nose. A pinpoint of cold hit her forehead. Another struck her cheek. She tilted her head back to see past the leaves of the cottonwood. The sky had gone gray. It was raining.

"Ellen?"

She spun around to see a tall man on a rangy pinto staring down at her. "Pa."

He dismounted and strode toward her. "Are you hurt? I was watching from up on the ridge. What in the dickens is going on?"

Helpless to explain, Ellen let her father hold her for a few minutes. Then they started home together, the bull dallied to her father's saddle, Ellen leading Deerfoot at a slow walk behind the cow. The rain stopped, then started again, a little harder. Ellen shivered as her shirt soaked through. It was beautiful to be cold, to be wet. Grampa was all right, and she had found the bull. Her father was home safe. The longest day of her life was finally over.

Grampa is so happy. Fay has had her foal, a pretty bay colt, born sometime last night. None of us knew until I went down to milk this morning. Dolly was licking it, too, like a fond aunt helping out with the new baby.

Grandpa says his head still hurts like blazes, but he was up out of bed this morning, helping Pa. All the cattle are in the west pasture now, until Pa can get a new sucker rod of white oak for the east pasture windmill. The bull still looks rough, but Pa says he will be fine after a few days of good feed and water. I hope so. Poor Deerfoot still looks tired. I suppose I do, too. I saw Pa give corn to Deerfoot this morning without me even having to ask.

Pa says he is proud of me. Grampa told him everything and said he should be glad he had me taking care of things instead of some hired man who wouldn't have cared half as much. Pa admitted it was true. Maybe now he will believe me when I tell him that I want to raise cattle. I know not very many women do it, but a few do. I can't see what's wrong with it. Maybe I will find a husband who wants a woman who knows how to help run a ranch.

Grampa gave me his riata. He says that from the way Pa described my roping, I am a better cowboy than he ever was—that I don't need a horse at all, just a cottonwood to dally my rope onto. He is only teasing, of course, but it makes me smile.

I love Grampa so much. I was so afraid when I first saw him on the ground. I hope I never have to feel that way again in my life.

Pa just walked out on the porch to look at the sky. I told him that I am going to make a roping stump out in the yard to practice on. He said he would help!

Spencer was at the door this morning, crying about the rain and his damp coat. He is the only creature in the world who was not joyous to see the rain. I spotted Murphy this morning, and she is slim as a rail again. As soon as I find where she has hidden her kittens, I will make sure to put milk close by so she doesn't have to leave them to beg milk on the porch.

Pa is calling that I had better get to bed. I expect he is right. There will be plenty of work tomorrow.